W9-BRY-174

PERMANENTLY WITHDRAWN
FROM
HAMMERSMITH AND FULHAM
PUBLIC LIBRARIES

nothing in sight

Translated by Kenneth J. Northcott

With an Introduction by Scott Denham

The University of Chicago Press · Chicago and London

nothing
in sight

jens rehn

Jens Rehn was born in Flensburg in 1918 and was a U-boat officer in World War II. In 1950 he became a journalist at the RIAS Berlin radio station and in 1958 was put in charge of the literature department. He died in Berlin in 1983. Kenneth J. Northcott is professor emeritus of German at the University of Chicago. He has translated a number of books for the University of Chicago Press, most recently SAID's *Landscapes of a Distant Mother*. Scott Denham is professor of German at Davidson College.

The University of Chicago Press, Chicago 60637
The University of Chicago Press, Ltd., London
© 2005 by The University of Chicago
All rights reserved. Published 2005
Printed in the United States of America

14 13 12 11 10 09 08 07 06 05   1 2 3 4 5

ISBN: 0-226-70734-2

Originally published as *Nichts in Sicht* in 1954 by Hermann Luchterhand Verlag. Reprint © Schöffling & Co. Verlagsbuchandlung GmbH, Frankfurt am Main 2003.

The publication of this work was supported by a grant from the Goethe-Institut.

LIBRARY OF CONGRESS CATALOGING-IN-PUBLICATION DATA

Rehn, Jens.
    [Nichts in Sicht. English
    Nothing in sight / Jens Rehn ; translated by Kenneth J. Northcott ; with an introduction by Scott Denham.
        p. cm.
    ISBN 0-226-70734-2 (cloth : alk. paper)
    I. Northcott, Kenneth J.   II. Title.
PT2678.E33N513 2005
833'.914—dc22   2004022681

⊗ The paper used in this publication meets the minimum requirements of the American National Standard for Information Sciences—Permanence of Paper for Printed Library Materials, ANSI Z39.48-1992.

HAMMERSMITH & FULHAM	
LIBRARIES	
011 770 32 3	
MAC	136138
	£13.00

Contents

Introduction

Scott Denham

*The boat had remained at periscope depth. In the meantime, it had
grown light. The two corvettes threw a few depth charges blindly
in the vicinity and then withdrew. It didn't seem to be all that
important to them.*

*And then, just as they had loaded new torpedoes, a passenger
ship hove into view in the periscope, a rag merchant, as these ships
were called. The rag merchants' job was to come along behind the
convoy to pick up the people who had been left in the water off the
ships that had been torpedoed the previous night.*

So, everyone back to battle stations. Attack.

*The ship was already in their crosshairs and was down at the
stern after the first torpedo struck it aft. The next torpedo struck
between the bridge and the smokestack. The ship broke in two and
quickly sank. There were a lot of people swimming in the water.
Not a pretty sight. The sea was very rough. The people could not
survive for long in the water.*

*When they had dived and were slowly sailing away, three de-
stroyers suddenly appeared. They were making straight for them.
The submarine dived quickly to maximum depth. "A plus 120," said
the chief officer, and directed the hydroplane guests with his fiddle
bow. "Now we're in for it."*

*In the hydrophones, they could hear the destroyers coming on
relentlessly. They were paying no attention to the people in the
water; instead they were attacking. They were old, experienced*

hands: now this could become interesting. Pick-pick, that was their
direction finder, their Asdic had picked up the U-boat and now the
first Brit was making his run to fire depth charges. He was being
damn accurate. "Full speed ahead both engines, hard-a-starboard,
fore half, aft below, five," came the command, and then the first
wave of depth charges exploded right above the boat and very close.
The water-level glasses shattered, the fuses fell out. And then the
next Brit approached, his screws could be heard plainly. Now he
was exactly overhead, the depth charges fell . . .

Did Jens Rehn witness this scene? Did he cause it, or one like
it? We don't know. Yet the picture is striking, the cool, objective
description is effective, the dying is real.

We do know that Otto Jens Luther, Jens Rehn's real name,
was a submarine officer and that his U-boat was sunk in 1943.
He was captured—or, better, rescued—and spent the rest of
the war in a British POW camp until his release in 1947. He
was born in Flensburg in the far north of Germany in 1918,
studied music, and then went to war. He published ten books
between 1954 and 1981 and also worked as an editor in radio all
his postwar life; he died in 1983 in Berlin. *Nothing in Sight* is
his only successful book and this scene is one of the very few
combat scenes Rehn ever published.

Nothing in Sight is a war novel, but there is not much war
in it. Instead we find only two characters, the "one-armed
man," a downed American fighter pilot, and the "other man,"
a German submarine officer. A battle at sea has left them both
stranded on a rubber life raft, floating alone in the midst of the
vast ocean, with nothing between them but a half a bottle of
whiskey, sixty-four cigarettes, a few chocolate bars, and some
chewing gum. The stage is thus set for hearing their conversations and their psychic and spiritual trials as they both move
toward death over the course of a few days. They are stranded
and they die, the one-armed man from infection, the other man
from thirst. That is all. The tale presents us with the minimal

interaction between the two men thus condemned and with the memories, dreams, and hallucinations of their last hours and days. In these two men's minds a much more lively drama is under way: a philosophical debate about the meaning of life, the existence of God, and the possibility of meaningful human relationships. So it is also much more than a war story.

The scene here comes to the reader through the dream of one of the two characters. Perhaps also from Rehn's own memory.

From 1950 on he worked for RIAS Berlin, one of the several Allied-sponsored media and propaganda outlets begun after the war. *Rundfunk im amerikanischen Sektor* (Radio in the American Sector) is the source of the acronym in both German and English. RIAS provided news, information, music and culture shows, and, increasingly radio plays and literary readings. Though initially under a fairly heavy Allied hand, the German media in the western zones rapidly became independent and served the new West German democracy well. Under the Nazis all the media—newspapers, publishing houses, radio, arts, culture, drama, literature—had all been completely co-opted by the regime. The Nazified press had to be replaced immediately after the war and the new radio stations played a key role in informing, educating, and entertaining the citizens, first of a completely shell-shocked society and then, after the founding of the two Germanies in 1949, of the new states. In the 1950s radio in the divided Germany played an especially important role in the recovering society on both sides of the political divide, and even more so after the Berlin Wall went up in August of 1961, for radio could be heard on both sides of the wall. Radio Bremen (in the British sector in West Germany) and RIAS in West Berlin were both known to have especially lively and daring literary productions in the 1950s and 60s. Rehn was instrumental in keeping RIAS on the cutting edge of culture and literature in West German radio. He became head of the culture desk in 1958 and ran the literary and cultural side of RIAS until his retirement in 1981.

Rehn began his public literary associations in the early 1950s through a loose circle of writers called the Group of 12, which met in Berlin every month or so in the apartment of one of the members. It was a low-key and flexible group, not limited to twelve—between ten and twenty would usually attend— and the goal was very simple: good, serious, no-nonsense writing. The members had no manifesto, no program, but sought simply to write straightforwardly, "without tricks." It was very much a workshop environment, collegial, informal, productive. Rehn played down his role in this group over the years, and it is not clear whether he was important in giving it direction. Still, it must have been fundamental to his development as a writer. The accolades that followed the publication of *Nothing in Sight* in 1954, including the Berlin Literary Prize for Young Authors, gave Rehn and his hard-boiled style the clout and affirmation they deserved. The direct and unadorned prose he wrote was a kind of salve for readers in postwar Germany, who were ready for new voices. The first reviewers raved at Rehn's fresh new voice and style. "A new man: Jens Rehn . . . an astounding debut." "Already more than a hope." "One need only read the first paragraph . . . to know that one is dealing here with a talented, self-disciplined author of the generation of writers tempered by the war; we can expect substantial things from him."

But Rehn was unable to repeat the performance of his first book, which remains an exception in his long, if modest, literary career. It seems that the novel has consistently found readers in the context of broader social concerns about war and death. It has had eight editions in German, including a book club edition and two paperback editions. The most recent was published in 2003 and was marketed in the German context of renewed interest in the suffering of Germans and German soldiers during World War II. In all, there have been some thirty thousand copies printed in German.

In 1955 the Luchterhand publishing house was so pleased with the success of *Nothing in Sight* that it immediately offered an advance on Rehn's next book. The publisher succeeded in placing a few foreign editions; translations appeared in Finnish (1955), French (1958), and Italian (1961). Despite attempts to find an English publisher in both Britain and the United States, no one was interested in Rehn. (Luchterhand's rising star at the time was Günter Grass, who went on to win the Nobel Prize for Literature.) The French reviews were especially enthusiastic, perhaps because of the novel's familiar existentialist tones and the fact that it did not feel like a typically Teutonic book. It lacked the heavy, self-important swirl of regime-friendly books of the decades before; it was neither the familiar "blood and soil" novel of individual struggle nor an abstract and lyrical neoromantic look inward. One French reviewer called it "the most notable German literary event of the last decade," that is, since the end of the war. For the French, Rehn was heir to the real German Romantics, such as Kleist and E.T.A. Hoffmann and their irony, but also to the symbolic prose of Hermann Broch, famous for his social-critical novel *The Sleepwalkers*. Rehn was "the Joseph Conrad of the age of Beckett," one reviewer said, a writer with the sensibility and penetrating brilliance of Camus and the realism of the war experience of Ernst Jünger (see below),whom the French have always admired.

Reviewers, both German and foreign, often found echoes of other writers' works and styles. The connections to Beckett are immediately apparent: a radically reduced stage that allows for two characters to delve into the philosophical paradox of life in the modern world. The existentialist concerns of Camus are present, too, and Hemingway comes to mind not only because of all that water, water everywhere and not a drop to drink, but also because of Rehn's own terse, direct, unadorned style. Rehn's was a war story—and was seen as such—but it was also an existentialist philosophical treatise on death. These two aspects of the story make it worth reading and rereading, even today, fifty years after its first publication.

If this was the new war story, it was being read in the grand context of a well-known German war literature born of the experience of the trenches in World War I, full of mud and pain and individual suffering and death for no good cause. The World War I experience was brought home most successfully through the severe irony that comes of the juxtaposition of ideas and reality. Erich Maria Remarque's Paul Bäumer rescues his wounded platoon leader and sergeant Kat at the end of *All Quiet on the Western Front* (1929) only to have him shot in the back of the head and killed as Paul carries him to safety. Arnold Zweig's sweeping tetralogy, the most famous novel of which is *The Case of Sergeant Grischa* (1927), tells the story of the absurdity of a military justice system grinding along as the world crumbles around it. In the Anglo-American tradition, Wilfred Owen turns Horace on his head by intoning "dulce et decorum est" across the gas-dying in the trenches, "yelling out and stumbling, and flound'ring like a man in fire or lime." German war poetry also had the violence of, for example, August Stramm (killed in 1915 at Gorodec): "the hour bleeds / Query raises the eye / Time births / Exhaustion / Rejuvenates / Itself / Death." The flood of First World War literature—literally hundreds of novels and thousands of poems, most somehow critical of the whole event—reached its high point around 1930. The Nazis quickly put an end to the negative views of the war experience, burning both Remarque's and Zweig's books in their bonfires in March of 1933, and allowed literary treatments of war to remain only if they satisfied either a crass kind of propagandistic need to glorify battle and sacrifice for the nation and the Volk, or if they treated the war as a kind of natural catastrophe that had to be faced by a lone individual. There were few of the latter sort of books, with the best known being those of Ernst Jünger (1895–1997), a highly decorated veteran of four years in the trenches, who first wrote a war memoir in 1921 and then revised and rarefied his representation of war in several similar books through the mid-1930s. His war stories glorified combat, aestheticized violence and death, and raised the experience of war to a kind of mythic rite of passage for young German men. Jünger's own right-wing, reactionary politics early on endeared him to the Nazis, but he was put off by their thugishness and had no interest in becoming a court author for Goebbels and Co., and so began to distance himself from the war drums by moving intellectually toward the existentialist thinking of Heidegger and Sartre. Jünger also penned a dark, mythical allegory against the Nazis in 1939, *On the Marble Cliffs*, which was read in opposition circles during the Second World War and nearly got Jünger into trouble with the regime. War becomes an existential confrontation for Jünger's individualistic hero.

Rehn's book was read, then, by Germans who knew both Remarque's critical, ultimately pacifist irony and Jünger's mythopoetic affirmation of violence as some kind of necessary natural event. Yet the war story that German soldiers carried in their packs in World War II was a thin little novella of the First World War by Walter Flex called *Wanderer Between Two Worlds*, a lyrical homage to camaraderie and loss, the story of two soldier friends, one of whom is killed in combat. Flex, a poet in the tradition of Hardy, or in the German context, of Detlev von Liliencron, published the story in 1917, just before he himself was killed in combat on the eastern front. The book became an immediate best seller during the war and went to sell millions of copies, second only to Remarque's *All Quiet*.

Wanderer was the one book that articulated for the average German the transcendental power of friendship, even love, between men in war, and the pain and loss when a buddy is killed. Flex's *Wanderer* was published in pocket editions even before the end of World War I and was on school reading lists throughout the 1930s (and even into the 1950s). It was popular, touching, and terribly well loved. It was mournful without being defeatist, nationalistic and patriotic without being rabid or racist. Flex gave spiritual meaning to sacrifice in battle. His buddy friendship endured beyond death.

There were other variations of war stories, of course, beyond these three types. Nazi propaganda novels glorifying sacrifice and demonizing the enemy are the most obvious, yet it is onto this triple-layered background of war literature that Jens Rehn painted his simple tale in 1954. Like Flex, Rehn presents a story of two soldiers in intimate proximity; like Jünger, Rehn moves the physical hardship of war to an existential level; and like Remarque, Rehn deploys irony to drive home his critical points. Yet aspects of Rehn's book are also very different and readers in 1954, who knew what to expect from a good war story, were excited about Rehn's new spin on these old tales. As in Flex's well-known novella, we find here too a duo, but this time they are enemies by assignment, allies by fate in their confrontation with death. As in Remarque, we find irony and an especially dark version of gallows humor, but the irony serves not to subvert the power structures of war—the grunts versus the generals and politicians away from the front. Instead Rehn gives us a kind of cosmic shrug of the shoulders and finds no meaning, rather than a political meaning, in the situation of his powerless soldiers. And as in Jünger's writings, the experience of war is mediated through a thorough knowledge of literary and philosophical existentialism in an attempt to take account of the experience of combat, suffering, and death. Yet Rehn does this without Jünger's purple prose and with a much finer brush.

Also unlike Jünger, Rehn gives a tight dramatic situation with a clear outcome and set dramatis personae. Finally, Rehn offers a popular version of contemporary discussions of God's indifference and impotence in the face of human suffering, something absent from all three of his predecessors and the trends in war writing that they represent. This is perhaps Rehn's most interesting achievement in *Nothing in Sight* and it connects the novel very directly to postwar, theologically grounded attempts at understanding and explaining the Holocaust.

The enthusiastic responses by Rehn's first readers had a lot to do with his ability to combine the best themes and tropes of the well-known war story genre. Readers found familiar ground on which to stand, but they were told to look in new directions. With nothing in sight on the horizon, Rehn directs our view inward, into his characters and their experiences, in an attempt to find meaning. There, he gives us not just nothing but nothingness.

As the one-armed man and the other man converse and dream and hallucinate, their minds continuously lead them to the conclusion that there is nothing of value or meaning in the world. They each reflect on their girlfriends, the one-armed man's Betsy and the other man's Maria, but find no meaning in those relationships.

> "The same result, fifty men dead. In two days it'll be fifty-one, counting me. C'est ça. Let's not talk about it. If I really get home again, I will get a wonderful medal, a very useful implement, especially out here. That'll be something for Betsy. It may even compensate for the arm, for the time being."
>
> "Betsy?"
>
> "My girl, Texas girl. Down there in Houston. Blonde like Lana Turner."
>
> "And?"
>
> "What, and?"

"I mean, and what else?"

The one-armed man threw his cigarette butt overboard. It went out with a tiny pop. It sounded like a distant shot.

"Nothing more. That's the damn thing that I've been made aware of today and yesterday. Because of my arm, you know."

Things simply are, or were, and that's that. C'est ça. Nothing more.

"Have you got a Betsy?"

"There were a lot of Betsys," said the other man. "But they don't count. The one that does count was Maria. She's dead."

"You see!" The one-armed man was satisfied that he was right. "That's just it. It has to be like that. Just at the point when there's some sort of a chance, that's when she goes and dies. In such good time that nothing comes of it, or at least only half of it does."

"It doesn't have to be like that, " said the other man.

"Yes, it sure as hell does."

The other man, the German, tries to hold on to his dead Maria and take solace in what she meant for him, but their own hopeless situation prohibits any kind of transcendence:

"Your Maria is the great exception, perhaps?"

"Leave it!"

"Maria is dead. All right. Finis amatae. The congregation rises to pray."

"Maria is not dead," said the other man distinctly. "You can die without being dead."

"A bridge, a bridge!" cried the one-armed man, and looked the other man straight in the eyes.

Here is the challenge of meaning: a bridge to what? To where? To whom? The quickly expiring one-armed man confronts the other man's insistent claims that his Maria meant something. The other man claims that it is one's own state of mind that really matters:

"And not only Maria. There are others as well. You don't always need to know them. It often depends upon oneself whether one knows the others."

"Thank you," said the one-armed man. "Thank you, I understand."

"No," said the other man quickly. "It's not like that. It's different. There was a whole lot that I didn't know before."

"I'm sorry," said the one-armed man. "You have to understand that I often like to be nasty now. It's a sort of therapy. A cut, like my arm. By the way, do you think that I like dying?"

"Yes," said the other man. There was nothing left for him to say.

"That's good." The one-armed man had grown quiet. "Of course I don't like dying, and neither do you."

But the inevitability of death cuts off their deliberations once again. Rehn contrasts over and over the beginnings of serious questions about the meaning of life with the basic trials of physical existence. Here, for example, toward the end of the first section, just before the one-armed man dies, he says:

"It only remains to ask about the 'meaning of it'!" said the one-armed man and shivered more violently. "The damn, childish, teenage question about the meaning of it: idiotic, wretched!" The shivering increased . . . he had no more time to feel exactly what was happening to him. The red wave rose up and ran on and into him. Its focal point fixed above the stump of his arm, in his shoulder and chest. The fire was feeling for his heart.

The question of meaning is carried along through the symbol of the woman Maria, the perfect woman. Her sudden death, for which the other man feels guilty, as if he had caused it in some way by loving her, cuts off his ability to have a meaningful relationship, we learn. Maria comes to stand for the other man's shattered dreams and expectations. In the conversation with the one-armed man, we see Rehn's cynicism in his critique of faith in an afterlife, or even in memory: "A bridge, a bridge!"

They claim to understand each other but are really talking past each other here and elsewhere. There are no bridges, no connections; there is no way out and nothing to hope for, and, we are told, even a memory of a relationship must be a false one.

Rehn's short novel is divided into five sections. The one-armed man dies at the end of the first, the other man heaves his body overboard at the end of the second, and then , over the next three sections, the other man slowly dies of thirst, becoming increasingly hallucinatory as thirst tortures him. The dead one-armed man remains part of the dialogue, though, by way of narrative flashbacks and dreams, prompted in the other man by the tenacious corpse floating along behind the rubber dinghy, just out of reach, but in sight, for a while. Between the conversations, both real and imaginary, the novel is organized in several other ways. Most obvious is Rehn's use of encyclopedia-style entries to address key concepts: how to amputate an arm, skin, thirst, God, stars, dreams, seawater, hope, hallucinations. These impersonal, objective entries generally occur as a caesura between day and night, or at the beginning a new section, and serve to mark a new focus of the story. Their scientific language serves to separate the reader from any kind of empathy toward the characters; instead they are viewed from a distance, objectively. Their fate becomes an object of interest and inquiry, but not of sympathy.

A further organizing tool is the use of tropes such as the relationships between the men and their girlfriends, a variation of this in the form of a semireligious Mary symbolism, the two men's attitudes toward their respective experiences before the war brought them together, and a symbolic structure arranged around sun, water, darkness, light, space, time, and aloneness.

If we look at the trope of the sun, for example, we see how it functions nearly like a character through its presence on the scene and how it interacts with, or acts upon, the others. The sun's rising and burning and setting mark time for the men on the ocean throughout the book. The sun is a classic trope with associations throughout world literature. Rehn uses the sun as a kind of deity, a visible substitute for God. At the same time, the sun represents all of nature in its indifference. Rehn also uses the sun as a symbol for God in his character's theological musings. In one hallucinatory moment the other man hears a voice:

> *The voice whispered.*
> *"You two, you'll not be found and you will be sailing through eternity with the dead man. The sun will melt you to pieces and you will merge and become one and the sun will fuse you together. Your flesh will melt away and your bones will become polished white and brittle with the heat, two skeletons in an embrace, for you belong together. Forever and ever. Ever."*

Almost like a funeral liturgy, the voice chants out the men's demise and future in death. For much of the story, especially after the one-armed man's death, the other man fights against the hopelessness of the situation, both practically, in terms of the immediate physical situation there in the boat, and spiritually, as he tries to find hope and meaning in the prospect of death. He reckons how much longer he can survive on the meager and inappropriate rations in the boat. He takes account of his life—does he owe anyone money, do people owe him?—and concludes his balance is not so bad. He repeatedly mourns the death of his girlfriend and tries to understand what her death meant and means, as he approaches his own. His conclusions are simple:

> *Yet the dead man said nothing. What else was he to do? Dead people never say anything. Dead people speak only through their presence in the feelings of others.*
> *The other man suddenly exploded:*
> *"I don't want you! Not you and not Maria or tomorrow and not myself either. When you're dead, it's all over. Finis. End."*

And then in the final lines of the story the sun plies its natural course through the sky, like the gods, indifferent to the living and dying going on below.

> *"The sun," he said softly and looked at the red, moistly pregnant ball. "The last sun, oh, well . . ."*
>
> *. . . The sun rose next morning, as it had been accustomed to do from time immemorial, and burned down on the motionless sea with all the strength at its disposal.*

And so the novel is a metaphor for the hopelessness of life. Rehn's parable of an indifferent God and helpless people ends with the inevitable, unavoidable state of things: there is nothing in sight.

Jens Rehn's literary work after *Nothing in Sight* continued to address the meaning of death and loss in a world with an indifferent God, at least in his next two novels. *Fire and Snow* (1956) is set in the last months of the war, in the winter of 1944–45 and follows a lone German survivor of one of the treks from the eastern provinces toward the west. As Germans fled in front of the Red Army's advance, they had to overcome not only the harsh weather, but also Allied air attacks. The Soviet army seemed to be the most deadly threat to the wagon trains of German farmers, old people, women, and children. However, the group of villagers Rehn portrays in his second novel is killed by falling through the ice as the line of carts and horses and people walking is strafed by an Allied airplane. All die except the narrator, whose story is an aimless and hopeless journey—first simply away from the site of all the death, then, together with his sturdy draft horse, back east, through days of driving snow and bitter cold. The man becomes disoriented and lost and ends up finally back at the place where he began, all the while musing and puzzling about the meaning of his life. This novel was followed in 1959 by *The Children of Saturn*, a parable set in the future after a nuclear war. Here again, Rehn asks readers to follow characters in extreme situations as they confront both physical trauma and death in their immediate situation, and the philosophical and theological implications of violent death for no reason.

Rehn said his first three novels were a trilogy of the war, and they have similar concerns. Only the first, with its dramatic situation reduced to the barest minimum, the two men in the boat and nothing else, and with the action limited to nothing but their impending and inevitable deaths, succeeds in bringing readers to the point Rehn is interested in showing us, the moment of complete existential despair, both in the context of the German Zeitgeist of the 1950s and beyond, timelessly and universally. Rehn's is a war story for all time.

nothing in sight

1

The swell had completely subsided. The sun was burning down on a dead calm sea. A light haze lay over the horizon. The rubber dinghy moved imperceptibly. The one-armed man kept a constant watch on the horizon. The other man was sleeping.

There was nothing in sight.

When an arm can no longer be nourished by the body, the skin peels off. The arm begins to suppurate and becomes gelatinous and discolored. It is advisable to operate quickly. Since the large blood vessels contracted when the arm was shot off, there is no danger of hemorrhaging. The frayed and jagged stump sticks out of the wound, a smooth bullet fracture. The procedure is fairly simple: the remaining muscles are separated with a circular cut, and the arm is then off. The wound is bandaged with half of the undershirt. Of course it goes on suppurating. The remains of the muscles also discolor, becoming mostly grey and green. The pain is at times severe. The lymph glands turn red and become as big as chicken's eggs. A racing pulse and violent shivering, shortage of breath and a dry mouth. And so it goes on. There is scarcely anything to be done.

"Give me another whiskey, it'll be time to stop work in a moment anyway," he said. "And throw the arm overboard for God's sake."

"How's the pain?"

"Good."

"Cigarette?"

The other man threw the arm overboard and gave the one-armed man a light. The arm sank very slowly and could be seen for quite a while in the clear water. They leaned far over and watched it until it had disappeared into the depths.

"There it goes and it will sing no longer," said the one-armed man and emptied his mug. A drop clung to the stubble on his chin and sparkled in the sunshine. The cigarette smoke clung motionless to their faces. A few wisps of seaweed floated across the water. The sky was cloudless. The horizon trembled in the heat. The sea lay like a board.

They each drank another shot of whiskey and then tried to go to sleep. The dinghy rocked gently as they moved around, trying to find a bearable position to sleep in. The one-armed man lay on his good side. The stump of his arm stood straight up towards the sky. His dreams moved beneath the stubble of his beard and his left leg twitched at times.

A rubber dinghy is about seven and a half feet long and four and a half feet wide. In proportion to this, the mid-Atlantic, at this point, is so large that the exact measurements make no difference.

When a rubber dinghy is floating on its own in the mid-Atlantic, it is immaterial whether it is drifting there in peace or war. The nationality of two people floating along alone in the mid-Atlantic, two people destined to die of thirst if they are not found in good time, is also of no consequence. The sun is not interested in whether the one-armed man is an American and the other man a German. And whether both of them are sitting in a rubber dinghy in the middle of the Atlantic in the year 1943. The sun merely radiates its thermal energy, rises, reaches its zenith, and sets again. The sea is dead calm and has no interest in who is floating on it. The mid-Atlantic remains large and the rubber dinghy remains small. The limits never change.

Meanwhile the arm lies on the seabed at a depth of about seven thousand feet, if it hasn't already been eaten by a fish.

Towards evening, the one-armed man woke up again. He felt a pain in his arm at the place where there was no longer any arm. The sky was a cardinal's robe spread wide. The sea was spread with watercolors.

He looked for his pack of cigarettes and then he couldn't light a match; his other hand was missing. He held the cigarette between his lips. His tongue lay woody and thick in his mouth. But he did not wake the other man. He was glad that the other man was there at all; he leaned forward and looked into his sleeping face. Only his forehead glistened. There were violet shadows in the hollows and folds of his face. His lips looked cracked. Like the bark of a pine tree, he thought. Or like the skin of a roast that has been burnt.

He took the cigarette out of his mouth and felt his own lips. They were the same. Broken and cracked.

You only ever notice something when you see it, he thought, and again he tried to strike the match. In vain. He clasped the pack between his knees, but his legs suddenly trembled so violently that the pack fell down. It just wouldn't work. He felt the cigarette paper provocatively smooth between his cracked lips.

He scanned the horizon. There was nothing in sight.

That's the way it is, he reflected. Betsy will be surprised that I've become a left-hander. I imagine she won't be surprised. Dulce et decorum est pro patria mori.

[3]

The other man had awakened with a start and looked around distractedly. His face went on sleeping until he realized where he was.

"Give me a light," said the one-armed man. "I can't strike the damn match."

"How many cigarettes do we actually have left?"

They counted. They still had sixty-four cigarettes. And a good half bottle of whiskey. And a few bars of Chocacola and some pieces of chewing gum. That was all. They hadn't found anything else in the rubber dinghy.

The other man gave him a light and then lit a cigarette for himself. The smoke did him good. He breathed deeply and grew a little dizzy.

The sky had gradually grown green. Light cumulus clouds lay on the horizon.

They drank their evening ration of whiskey. The liquid did not seem to get half as far as their stomachs; it was as though it had already been absorbed by their dry tongues.

The one-armed man's stump was once again standing straight up from his body. The other man wanted to tell him to put his arm back down again; the unnatural position irritated him. Better not to, he thought, people are difficult when something's wrong with them. So he said only,

"How's the arm?"

"It's throbbing. They've got to find us soon. We're already thirty-six hours overdue. They've got our last position. There's just a stupid ache in my shoulder."

"Let me have a look."

"And I tell you what, they've long ago given up on us and they're not looking for us any more."

The other man examined the stump.

The edges of the wound had eaten further into the healthy flesh. The bandage was soaked with pus.

The other man took the other half of the undershirt and

bandaged the wound up again. Then he washed out the old bandage. The water was tepid and enveloped his hands like jelly. The pus had eaten its way into the fabric and could not be dissolved in the water. The other man turned pale and felt his stomach heave. But the nausea passed.

Everything will pass, he said to himself, and once more felt his hands in the soft, tepid water. A strange, rather kitschy saying that he had read somewhere—heaven knows where— came to mind: " . . . and our harsh, wet, human existence slips through our hands."

That was back then, when Maria was weeping in his hands. A day before she fell from her horse and broke her neck. But then of course it was too late. Now the tears were always in his hands. Wet hands soon begin to grow cold, especially when the water comes from tears.

At first it had not been at all easy, God knows. Maria had been lucky, for then, at least, there were hands into which she could weep. But he? Later? There had not even been a horse gracious enough to throw him at the right moment. So that he could break his neck and put an end to everything.

Of course he was to blame. How easily one gets to the point of being to blame. Even if Maria was to blame, he still felt guilty. That was an ingenious arrangement on God's part.

Often, when he had been especially despairing, he had still been able to feel her face in his hands. The soft, gentle, weeping something. And her mouth on the tips of his fingers when she sobbed.

Actually, he could have been happy now. Now that everything was coming to a close. Now that the horse was about to throw him. It had probably already thrown him. He was already off the horse and had not yet broken his neck. That well-known uncertainty.

Suddenly things were not nearly so simple, nor did he find

the relief he had always imagined he would. "Relief," that sounded good. Then would I be better off going on with freezing cold hands? To be found under the word "cowardice" in the dictionary? Life is like that. Poor Maria. "Poor," yes, that was also a useful sort of word. You always look into the mirror, no matter where you are.

And then the kitschy saying about wet human existence. Ah, well!

At the same time, he was convinced that Maria had not wanted to break her neck. But it had happened, and he sat there with his freezing cold hands.

The two men crouched down opposite each other on the narrow side of the dinghy. They saw each other only as dark shadows. Only where their faces must have been was it a little lighter. Occasionally when they looked up at the starry sky, the nocturnal light made their eyes and mouths more distinct. In the darkness their outlines were larger and came closer to each other. They sat motionless on the thick rubber padding.

It was pleasantly cool and they had put their jackets on again. The one-armed man had stopped too soon when putting his on; his missing arm was clearly visible. He had tucked the empty sleeve of his jacket carefully into his side pocket. The stump still stood out horizontally from his body. As though he had a handle, the other man thought.

They were less thirsty. The smoky taste of the whiskey lingered bitter in their mouths and the alcohol buzzed in their blood.

They each ate a bar of Chocacola. The sound of their teeth cracked from the inside of their mouths, against their ears, and sounded loud in the silence all around them. The glow of their cigarettes cast small, gentle lights up on to their faces. But they said nothing. They merely tried to smoke as slowly as they possibly could.

[6]

The horizon could no longer be made out exactly. The night had blurred and sucked out the only dividing line. The sea was dead calm. There was nothing in sight.

"They have to find us tomorrow!" said the one-armed man.

"If we are careful, the rations will last for another two days."

"Two days. By then my arm will have eaten me up."

"One of our U-boats must be somewhere in the neighborhood."

"Two days are too long. I know that. Eighth semester in medical school." The one-armed man grinned. "A nice end. Thanks!"

"Our boats all have a doctor on board," said the other man hesitantly.

"We shouldn't have attacked. Then you could have gone on."

"If and but."

"The same result, fifty men dead. In two days it'll be fifty-one, counting me. C'est ça. Let's not talk about it. If I really get home again, I will get a wonderful medal, a very useful implement, especially out here. That'll be something for Betsy. It may even compensate for the arm, for the time being."

"Betsy?"

"My girl, Texas girl. Down there in Houston. Blonde like Lana Turner."

"And?"

"What, and?"

"I mean, and what else?"

The one-armed man threw his cigarette butt overboard. It went out with a tiny pop. It sounded like a distant shot.

"Nothing more. That's the damn thing that I've been made aware of today and yesterday. Because of my arm, you know."

"I'm sorry," said the other man.

They fell silent again.

The Southern Cross had risen and stood clear and lovely above the low clouds on the horizon.

Houston is in the state of Texas on the navigable river Buffalo-Bayou, thirty miles from its mouth in Galveston Bay. There is an fifty-mile-long ship canal to the Gulf of Mexico.

Houston is an important railroad junction and a center of the cotton trade and the oil industry. The city is spacious and built in the modern style. Its climate is very hot and dry.

Mr. Benton was the owner of several automobile repair workshops and was a rich man. He was a widower and drank a lot. Almost everyone drinks here. The women as well. Because of the climate. He spent his weekends over in Florida, mostly with girls who were no older than his daughter Betsy. He was crazy about the Grieg piano concerto and he read the comics first in the newspaper. Recently he had been having stomach trouble and was not sleeping very well. By and large, he was easy to get along with and good-natured.

Betsy got to know William at college. Later they had become engaged. That's the way things are. It had been very romantic. However, William wanted to finish medical school before they got married. An old-fashioned point of view. In fact, Betsy really had enough money.

When she saw William in his airman's uniform for the first time she was very proud. Now that the war had started, she was suddenly mad to have children. When she got the phone call saying that he was missing, she wept and was sad. In the evening, at the party, she naturally told everyone and naturally started crying again. The people were all very considerate and comforted her.

In her pain, she drank rather a lot. It was only towards morning that she went home with Jim. She drove very fast and Jim was sleeping in the seat next to her. His teeth gleamed yellow in the early light. That irritated her and so as they rounded a curve the car went off the road and turned over. Jim died on the spot. In the hospital her leg—which had been completely

shattered—was taken off. When she came to from the anes-
thetic, she said nothing and made a childish attempt at suicide,
which was, of course, unsuccessful. In the evening her father,
who had come over from Florida at once, sat by her bedside.

"If William comes back," she said and wept unceasingly.
"Take it easy," said Mr. Benton. What else could he say?

The next morning, there was an all-around improvement
in his daughter's condition and he was able to take the second
early flight to Miami Beach.

In the late morning twilight, the Southern Cross stood clear
and lovely above the concrete runway.

Towards morning, the stars hung in a flat arc. The two men
were not sleeping. The coolness felt good. Their skin felt damp
all over. They were not hungry. They chewed gum only to pass
the time. But they soon spat the gum out; chewing it was too
hard on their salivary glands, which were swollen and painful.
So better not. They would keep the chewing gum in case, after
all, it did take longer, and they were to get hungry. For there
were only five bars of Chocacola left.

"They have to find us tomorrow!" said the one-armed man.
"If it weren't for this damned arm, I could stand it for quite
a time. But like this? Check my pulse will you?" The other
man counted. He had to hold his wristwatch close to his eyes.
It was exactly 5:17 a.m. He felt the beating of the strange pulse
with the tips of his fingers. "Hundred," he said; he had counted
120.

It was now 5:18 a.m. A hundred and twenty pulse beats had
passed. One hundred and twenty. "Please write out in words"
always appeared on checks and on bills.

He held on to the one-armed man's arm as if he were going
to go on counting. The skin of his wrist felt dry. Of course it
could be his own skin that was dry. But the one-armed man
had a fever. Pulse rate, 120. So it was probably his skin that was

[9]

dry. One hundred and twenty, it shouldn't be more than that, he thought. But there's nothing we can do about it. They have to find us tomorrow without fail.

There was nothing in sight.

The one-armed man's teeth began to chatter. His forehead was hot. The fever and the shivers came over him in strange waves. The shivering began down below in his legs and then rose like water through his whole body. When the wave arrived at his shoulders, the stump of his arm moved and stretched. When this happened, the one-armed man always made a noise with his teeth, as though a rough file were scraping the edge of a piece of sheet metal. But the one-armed man did not cry.

The other man kept on talking rapidly. He did not know what he should or could say, he could not find coherent words. He also had no time to search for the right words. He saw that it didn't matter what he said: the one-armed man couldn't understand him in any case. So he just said whatever came into his head. Rapidly and loudly and without interruption.

When the one-armed man suddenly stopped shivering and collapsed, the other man went on talking for a moment; he was not able to stop so suddenly.

And once more there was a vast silence.

The sun had risen. It was already a finger's width above the horizon when the other man noticed it. The one-armed man was unconscious. But he had not cried out. Now, that's worth imitating, thought the other man. Well done! And then he grew afraid that the one-armed man might perhaps be dead. He slid over to him and put his ear to his chest. But his heart was beating. It was even beating regularly and peacefully, almost a little too slowly. He took hold of the arm that was left and took his pulse.

"Ninety; oh, well."

The warmth of the sun became more noticeable. He could see that it was now at least eight degrees above the horizon.

The sky was absolutely clear and cloudless. The sea was covered with a light haze and reflected like mercury.

The one-armed man's unconsciousness must meanwhile have changed into sleep, for when he awoke he felt fresh and almost free of pain.

"How was it?" the one-armed man asked, and was afraid.

"How are you?" the other man asked in reply, and added hurriedly, "What do you think about breakfast?"

He poured out a third of a mugful of whiskey and passed it across. It took the one-armed man a little time to realize that he had to take it with his left hand. The stump always made a slight reflex movement at first. But the other man already knew that and looked away in good time.

Alcohol does not sit well on an empty stomach. The other man vomited and quickly ate a bar of chocolate.

"Take another slug," said the one-armed man. "And keep it in your mouth, then the sick feeling will go away."

But the other man did not want to. It took a long time for the taste of bile to go away.

They took their jackets off again. The sun burned down from the sky at an angle and the heat increased with each heartbeat. They peeled strips of dried skin off their bodies, and it was a sort of game: when one or the other succeeded in peeling off an especially large and undamaged piece they held it up to the light. They saw beautiful graining and patterns in their skin. They had not known before what lines and figures they carried around with them on their skin.

"Strange," said the other man, "strange what you see and notice now."

The one-armed man kept silent and no longer took pleasure in his skin.

A human being's skin is thinner and, for the most part, less hairy than that of other mammals and, depending on the situation, varies greatly in thickness. Thus, the dermis on the eyelid is only about 0.5 mm. thick, while on the sole of the foot it is 2 or 3 mm. thick, the subcutaneous cell tissue on the head is 0.6 to 2 mm. and on the rest of the body 4 to 9 mm. thick; in the case of a fat person it can be up to 30 mm. thick. The outer skin protects the body from mechanical injuries and harmful external effects. By means of the sense organs contained in it (sense of heat and cold, sense of direction, sense of touch, sense of space) it conveys impressions of the most diverse sort.

If a person loses more than one third of his skin surface, usually he dies. In early, uncultivated times human skin was a favorite material for the making of articles of jewelry and similar objects, and in order to retain its pliancy the skin was stripped from one's captured enemies while they were still alive. This custom is no longer practiced in Western culture.

There was a red glow at the places where they had peeled off the burnt skin. The new skin felt silky and like parchment. It was pleasant to stroke the place with one's finger.

A Portuguese-man-of-war passed slowly by on the starboard side. The triangle of its back, erect in the air, shimmered light blue and mauve, its tentacles pointed gently down into the depths. It was beyond their range. Otherwise there was nothing in sight.

"Dinner gong," said the one-armed man after they had been looking at the jellyfish for some time. "It's noon."

They each ate a bar of Chocacola. They tried diluting their shot of whiskey with a little sea-water, so as to eke out their ration. But it tasted so awful that they decided not to try experiments like that in the future. The salt burned their mouths. The peppermint taste of the chewing gum, thank God, took away some of the bitter taste.

They tried to sleep, taking turns so as not to miss the plane.

But they had difficulty in sleeping. The heat and the thirst and the arm left them no peace.

They dozed. But one of them would often sit up and scan the horizon.

Finally they fell asleep.

The one-armed man dreamed about playing the piano and of a lot of ice-cold bottles of soda water.

A bottle of soda water costs five cents in the United States, in Germany, twenty pfennigs. Whiskey tastes best with just a splash of soda and is kept cool with ice-cubes. Of course, old men like to drink their whiskey neat. Between sips, it is nice to eat a pretzel to keep the taste buds awake.

Back then, when they had been celebrating passing their preclinical exams, they had drunk whiskey without soda. It had been a wild booze-up, and the girls had told them wonderful jokes about their anatomy class.

He could not remember the end of that night. When he woke up next morning, he saw Betsy lying next to him, bloated and passed out. It was the first time that he hadn't liked her. And then, when he looked in the bathroom mirror, he was frightened by the sight of his own face. He looked worse then Betsy. Besides which, he had an unbearable headache. He was incapable of doing anything all morning and had done nothing but drink soda water.

The one-armed man swallowed and licked his lips with his dried-out tongue without finding anything. The other man was fast asleep and had turned his back to the sun. He had squeezed his face into the space between the bottom of the dinghy and the rubber padding.

And Maria was alive and he was with her somewhere, and they were swimming and the sun had just risen and they were shouting in the water because it was so beautiful, and then she felt a little cold and he rubbed her and she liked it, and then they had breakfast in the garden and the birds were singing, my God, they were singing, and the speckled chicken pecked food out of Maria's hand, and the jam sparkled red in the sunshine and everything was unbelievable and wonderful, and he breathed deeply and kept looking at Maria and she was acting as though she didn't notice, and a year later she was dead.

They drank their evening shot and smoked down the cigarettes they had been smoking at noon until they burned their lips. They did not have many cigarettes left.

The sun was a giant red ball and had already half disappeared into the water. It felt as though there might be dampness in the air.

In front of them, a swarm of flying fish shot out of the water. The sudden noise was like a little shock. Shortly afterwards, they saw the dolphins that were chasing the fish. Their bellies shone pink in the sun when they rolled over, snorting. Otherwise there was nothing in sight.

"If you know a little about medicine, you know too much," said the one-armed man. He was sitting on the bottom of the dinghy and was leaning against the rubber padding. He put his one hand in the water, lifted it up, and looked at the water dripping off it. But it was an effort for him and he soon stopped.

"They'll come tomorrow," said the other man. He noticed that the stump was no longer sticking straight up. It was hanging down a little, but not much.

"Look!" the one-armed man sat up straighter. "It's so terribly sticky . . ."

The other man unbandaged the stump. It did not look good and it stank. The putrefaction had spread to the armpit. Tomorrow would really be the very last day.

The one-armed man looked very closely at the remains of his arm.

"Give me a cigarette," he said.

As the other man was bandaging him up again with the half of the undershirt that he had washed out, the one-armed man gave a little cry: the other man had touched the stump on the inside and the shock had gone through all the other bones in his body. And now there was something the matter with them as well, he could feel that quite plainly.

"There's nothing more to be done," he said. "If it had at least been a shot low down on the arm, then I would have some reserve in the upper arm. But like this? Classic case. Curtains, Professor!"

He had slipped further down again. The other man fastened the bandage with a safety pin.

"I think my temperature is going up again," said the one-armed man and his eyes had begun to blink rapidly. "Take my pulse again."

The other man took his pulse. He found it at once.

"And hit me if I start to do something silly!" said the one-armed man and kept blinking his eyes faster and faster.

The other man had miscounted and started again from the beginning. "A hundred and seven," he said after a minute. But it had been a hundred and twenty-seven.

"When does it get critical?" he asked him.

"After a hundred and thirty." The one-armed man held himself tight.

The other man wet the bandage that had been washed and laid it on the one-armed man's forehead. The undulating movements had started again. The stump was describing little conic circles.

Meanwhile, the sun had disappeared beneath the horizon. The sky had turned into a vast red tomato. It was growing dark along the horizon, which was delineated as sharp as a knife.

It would be better for him if he were to die quickly, the other man thought. He's tormenting himself and I'm going to crack up in the process.

The other man did not know what he could do. So he did nothing, he just waited and watched. He reapplied the wet bandage from time to time, but it wasn't much help, apparently. The one-armed man was breathing spasmodically and was saying words that were incomprehensible. He was talking so quickly that it sounded like short bursts of machine-gun fire. His face had disappeared completely under the stubble of his beard. Only his nose stuck out sharply from his sunken face. He kept his eyes shut.

"I wonder what he can see," the other man asked himself, and remembered the horizon. He took a quick look around.

The dinghy rocked gently under the movements of the one-armed man. The water lapped under the bottom of the dinghy like a gourmand eating oysters.

The one-armed man was grinding his teeth and the other man could find no escape from the grating noise. Then his lower jaw fell feebly down and shook. His open mouth was larger than usual.

When the one-armed man's jaws were about to snap shut again, the other man put the loose end of a thick piece of rope into his mouth. Biting on it did the one-armed man good and he exhaled forcefully through his nose in relief.

Things finally quieted down and they relaxed.

"Good, eh?" said the one-armed man and he could start thinking again. The other man gave him half a cigarette.

They waited for things to start up again, but they didn't.

Their sun-warmed bodies began to grow cold; night had fallen quickly. A scarcely perceptible breeze blew out of the northwest and took away the smell of pus.

They lay down next to each other, the other man on the healthy side of the one-armed man.

[16]

They looked up at the sky. Mars was straight ahead and sparkled red. The one-armed man looked for Venus but could not find it.

The starry sky on the ceiling of the bar was the only attraction. Although God knows it was a decent bar. They had returned an hour before from reconnaissance over the Atlantic and had nearly cracked up on landing. Bobby was dead and they hadn't managed to catch the U-boat; what a mess. Now they were celebrating, so to speak, and were grabbing at the barmaids.

Of course this was a decent bar. The people who were sitting around all had much too much money. He had come here with the boys direct from the airfield; they could feel Bobby, dead, in their bones. When the U-boat's flak had hit them and cut right through the plane, Bobby had suddenly lost the back of his head. It was not a pretty sight. And so they were boozing. Under the bar's starry sky. The good citizens with lots of money clapped them on the shoulders and bought drinks for their stylish heroes. And the little Babylonian houris offered themselves. What more could you want?

Later on, they'd had a fight with a fat wholesale grocer. The guy had a voice like a blob of fat floating on the soup, round and soft and oily. Fridolin had beaten the man up, quickly and painfully, but they were able to get away in plenty of time before the military police arrived.

Meanwhile, outside it had started raining and the stars had disappeared. The sky was like a thick sack. To hell with it, where shall we go now? He hadn't even wanted to write to Betsy.

"It's very strange," said the one-armed man, "when you know it will soon be all over. You at least still have a chance. I don't begrudge you that."

"What difference do a few days make?" The other man felt for the cigarettes.

"You only ever really know something when you no longer have any time left. And I'm really not scared, really not."

The match flared up, but its light could not compete with the starlight. The other man hastened to put it out. "I would really like to know why I studied medicine and why I insisted on becoming a doctor."

"Well," said the other man, without surprise.

"All that stuff about helping mankind is, of course, nonsense. You don't repair a car when it's not worth repairing. And most of them aren't worth it."

Silence.

"A few surgeons and some dentists would probably be enough. The best thing is to maintain your car properly. And to buy a decent make in the first place."

"Mine is at home on blocks, no gasoline."

"But I still don't know." The one-armed man was thoughtful. "Perhaps it's just not worth my getting to know. Perhaps it's just enough that you've done the wrong thing, and that you notice it at all later on. Like I did with Betsy, for example."

"Perhaps Betsy really is different, if she has no more time," said the other man, and he already knew what the one-armed man would reply.

"People always have too much time. And Betsy is . . . well, you can imagine what she's like. One of the really dangerous sort."

Neither of them spoke.

"Good grief," said the one-armed man, suddenly excited. "Just imagine, if I'd lived another thirty years and had married her and hadn't known all that and had become a doctor or something else, it doesn't matter, it's all the same."

"Come on, forget about the doctors," said the other man.

"But there is no better example." The one-armed man laughed wickedly. "They incorporate everything in themselves.

I know them, God knows. Get ten doctors drunk and listen to what they say about their patients."

"All of them?"

"Certainly. I'm a specialist, and it all comes back to me. Of course not all of them. She is the exception."

The other man wanted to get him off the subject. But he couldn't. "Just imagine!" the one-armed man went on, and was already beginning to die a little without being aware of it. "Just imagine: Mrs. Betsy and I and a car and two dear little children and Sunday afternoon and a successful career and a whole lot of money! Every day you tell yourself a pack of lies and think that everything is OK!"

Neither of them said anything and they both lit a cigarette. The other man counted and reported, "We have thirty-six left."

The one-armed man did not answer and just went on smoking. He sat lost in thought for a long time.

"Have you got a Betsy?"

"There were a lot of Betsys," said the other man. "But they don't count. The one that does count was Maria. She's dead."

"You see!" The one-armed man was satisfied that he was right. "That's just it. It has to be like that. Just at the point when there's some sort of a chance, that's when she goes and dies. In such good time that nothing comes of it, or at least only half of it does."

"It doesn't have to be like that, " said the other man.

"Yes, it sure as hell does."

They saw a swarm of shooting stars flash across the sky. In the far distance a dolphin barked once but not again, they waited in vain. The dinghy had turned around and Mars was now behind them; they could no longer see it. It was now Orion that stood with one foot on the horizon.

"Pain?"

"No," said the one-armed man, lying.

The other man was hungry and the chewing gum helped. It was cool.

And he remembered the autumn afternoon. He had wanted to meet Maria, but she couldn't get away, her boss wouldn't let her go. He had strolled through the harbor and he hadn't felt like doing anything. He'd watched the anglers on the quay leaning on the bollards staring morosely at their corks as they floated on the water. It had smelled of horizon, and distance, and longing.

In one corner of the harbor there was a large houseboat. It was called *The Flying Dutchman* and was a floating restaurant. He was hungry and ordered himself some plaice. He could look at the water through the porthole.

While he was separating the ivory-colored flesh from the bones, he looked at his plate; how good it looked! The creamy, rich yellow of the potato salad and the completely different, southerly yellow of the lemon rind; the lush green of the parsley shining shamelessly and laughing, with its curly scent of the garden, the rust red and olive green of the fish skin, with its precise red dots, already crisp on the edges where it had been up against the pan, how soft and silky was the flesh that lay beneath it, gleaming with the damp, tender and yet solid and well-arranged: it tasted so good. Heaven help us, it melted in your mouth!

He cleaned his plate, had coffee afterwards, and treated himself to an exquisite cognac with it.

The one-armed man had been quiet, as though he had been listening. He was panting.

"In pain?" the other man asked again.

"It's OK." And then after a pause, "This rabbit world!" The one-armed man's voice rose. "This rabbit world. It sleeps with its eyes open! I mean the others as well, not just my esteemed professional colleagues. These digestive giants. Digestion is everything, good digestion. The main thing is that the glands function properly!"

It seemed as though the one-armed man was speaking incoherently. But the subject intrigued the other man. He winced.

"And my wallet," he shouted.

"That's gland number one!" The one-armed man grew excited again. "Approved! Gland number two is four hands-breadth under the heart."

"All right, that's enough, leave it at that."

"Your Maria is the great exception, perhaps?"

"Leave it!"

"Maria is dead. All right. Finis amatae. The congregation rises to pray."

"Maria is not dead," said the other man distinctly. "You can die without being dead."

"A bridge, a bridge!" cried the one-armed man, and looked the other man straight in the eyes.

"And not only Maria. There are others as well. You don't always need to know them. It often depends upon oneself whether one knows the others."

"Thank you," said the one-armed man. "Thank you, I understand."

"No," said the other man quickly. "It's not like that. It's different. There was a whole lot that I didn't know before."

"I'm sorry," said the one-armed man. "You have to understand that I often like to be nasty now. It's a sort of therapy. A cut, like my arm. By the way, do you think that I like dying?"

"Yes," said the other man. There was nothing left for him to say. "That's good." The one-armed man had grown quiet. "Of course I don't like dying, and neither do you."

They both remained silent again for a long time. They each smoked another whole cigarette. It no longer mattered how many cigarettes they had, how they shared them, or whether there would be any left.

"And yet it might have been good and nice!" began the one-armed man again. "If only it weren't for this wretched arm. It simply means I have no chance any more." He laughed again. "A wonderful conversation, eh? Two men in a boat. Refrigerator-man and thinker-plus-poet's-grandchild. Nice little problems. We have nothing better to do. Great! Time is money, per aspera ad astra. Let him have it!"

The other man noticed that the stump of the arm was moving on the other side.

"Two men in a boat. That's it exactly! And now stop talking nonsense."

"I keep on asking you to excuse me," said the one-armed man. "I've never been in a situation like this before."

"We're just talking, aren't we? Or?"

The one-armed man shook himself again and the other man grew alarmed. Was the fever returning?

"Noted!" said the one-armed man and sat up straight. "Noted, from now on I will talk the standard language! We are very polite, French and modern and fecal: it's all "la merde!" No dots to spare maidens and aesthetes. Written out in full. What do you say about that?"

The other man also sat up.

They smoked another cigarette. The shivers and the fever began to take hold again. They each drank a shot of whiskey. The liquor ran like a sheet of flame into their stomachs. It went straight into the bloodstream and produced a light pressure on the eyes.

"Isn't that great?" The other man spoke quickly to distract the one-armed man. "I didn't let you drown when you were in the water. So, dots, with or without maidens, that's something quite different!"

"It only remains to ask about the 'meaning of it'!" said

the one-armed man and shivered more violently. "The damn, childish, teenage question about the meaning of it: idiotic, wretched!"

The shivering increased.

"Stop, I beg you, so no dots after all. And now watch out, it's starting again. Give me the rope!"

He wedged his legs under the bottom of the dinghy and took hold of the rope, which was used to haul people on board the dinghy, tightly in the crook of his arm. By then he had no more time to feel exactly what was happening to him. The red wave rose up and ran on and into him. Its focal point fixed above the stump of his arm, in his shoulder and chest. The fire was feeling for his heart.

The other man also began to shiver. He wedged his feet under the bottom of the dinghy. The butt of his cigarette stuck to his upper lip.

Until the one-armed man flipped out. He screamed out loud, a long drawn-out scream. The scream rose from the dinghy out over the sea and clung to the surface of the water all around.

The other man was sweating and dripping. The moisture ran down into the stubble of his beard. His face was freezing cold. He knew the feeling.

The one-armed man was raging. He bit the rope. The other man took his pulse. He counted a hundred and thirty five. But he was not sure whether that was right, because the one-armed man was flailing about so much.

Finally it was over. The one-armed man had fallen over as though someone had hit him. His face showed no sign of consciousness and glistened ill and white under his beard. The other man tore the cigarette butt from his lip and it hurt. The paper had stuck to the skin. He licked the place where it hurt and was surprised that his tongue was moist. Up till then, it had been dry.

With or without dots, he thought bitterly, and there was no one there that he could have killed. With or without dots. La merde. Not just what was here, but something completely different as well. And a great deal more, even. The substance, my dear friend. You never know something until you have no more time. The soul is broken. That nice little human soul. For a long time now. That's right. Just that. And if there is really anything left, really, then what is left gets smaller and smaller.

"La merde!" he cried.

But there was nothing in sight.

He sat down, exhausted. He would have liked to weep, but he couldn't.

He knew that none of it was true. And that the one-armed man had two arms. A crazy dream. Betsy, too, had a place where one could rest in spite of everything.

The doctors were not interested, and why wasn't Maria here? Now he was alone and his face was freezing cold. Wasn't it enough that his hands were? No one was there and the one-armed man couldn't do anything about it, he had the pain in his arm and would soon die.

The other man stood up. He saw Orion directly in front of him. He couldn't raise his arms and could think only about the one-armed man, whose scream still rang in his ears.

He looked up even higher than the stars and said, softly and dangerously:

"You," he said, "You up there. When I get hold of you!"

God (abstract: divinity) is the personified epitome of holiness, philosophically, the highest being. The genesis of the concept of God can be traced back to several roots within primitive religions. The essence of God can be determined only by reference to the world in the broadest sense. If we emphasize the contrast between that essence and everything that is known, then we arrive by negation (via negationis) at the "characteristics" of God, which become, in the final analysis, an empty abstraction. If we enhance known characteristics into the absolute (via eminentiae), then we cannot get beyond metaphorical language, the limits and justice of which are the object of dogmatic study.

Since the second century AD, attempts have been made to substantiate the existence of God by using the truth of the idea of divinity as proof.

We now prefer to speak of a regular interaction of final causes in which the unified, fundamental cause becomes apparent to us. The teleological proof is made in such a way that we can conclude the existence of a reasonable creator from several symptoms of divine order, intention, and purpose. This proof has been continued with many variants and further developments up to the present day. According to the current view there is, even today, a double significance attached to the proofs of the existence of God: on the one hand, there is that of a thoughtful portrayal of the way in which the idea of God enters clearly into one's consciousness, or on the other, that of a justification of the belief in God, and so of religion, in the face of the intellectual conscience.

The other man kept silent and the One-up-above did not answer.

The other man looked at Orion again more closely and it was unchanged and the one-armed man, too, lay unchanged. The night was dark blue, the sea dead calm. The other man lit a cigarette. The little point of flame took a little of the solitude away.

When dawn started to break, the one-armed man awoke. He was weak and very exhausted. The other man gave him a shot of whiskey and held out a cigarette to him.

The upper edge of the sun broke over the horizon and the

one-armed man raised himself up. He stood up without help. The other man knew that the one-armed man had to stand up on his own.

The sun's fiery light grew rapidly above the horizon. The one-armed man had raised his good arm and the remains of his other arm. He stood there black against the red and yellow sky and sang his great cantata of pain.

Before the song was finished, he died. He died quickly and still standing up.

He had already been dead for some time as he lay on the bottom of the dinghy.

2

The one-armed man was dead. His heart was no longer beating. His pulse had stopped. It no longer mattered whether it was one hundred twenty, one hundred thirty, or one hundred forty-six. Pulse beats had become meaningless. What, after all, was a number? If there was nothing to count? Simply go on counting, when there was no substance present?

The other man pondered and simply did not know what might be lying in store for him. But he felt that something was being prepared. The dead man lay there, it began to grow light, and the temperature was still comfortable.

The one-armed man had died. He had had to die, sooner or later. Because of his arm. But the other man was healthy, no shot and no wound. Just a bit thirsty. What was that compared with the one-armed man? Nothing. Everything all right. Please! At some point an aircraft would come, or a U-boat.

The sun rose over the horizon and there was nothing in sight.

The dead man lay in the opposite corner of the dinghy. His legs were in a strangely unnatural position. He should have laid his legs down differently before he died, the other man thought. But it all happened too quickly. He hadn't had enough time.

He is dead, he said to himself. He is no longer alive, he simply doesn't exist any longer. What's left here is only the shell, the remains, as empty as a box. A shame, I liked him very much. I should have met him earlier, a few years before this raft. And now? Are things better for him or are they better for me?

He pushed the dead man's legs into another position. Good, the sight was now more bearable.

"The dead always want something from the living," he said to himself. "When they are no longer alive their remains become independent and aggressive. Not just the one-armed man here, but the others as well. Even when they are already underground. Or under the water."

He thought about what he had just said for a long time and then repeated it. It was hard to get through this. But the fact remained that they did attack. Yes, they often bothered you. Just like the legs. Or as Maria did earlier. They give you no peace. Perhaps that's a sort of dead man's revenge? And what will the one-armed man do?

But the one-armed man was not bothered with the other man's thoughts. He lay still and almost friendly on the other side of the dinghy and was simply dead. Nothing more than that. It was enough just to lie there in front of him.

"In front," thought the other man. "My God, what is 'in front' here?" Was he in front or was the dead man in front? Who was on which side? Where were they headed? In what direction was the current flowing? Forward!

The other man could not determine what was in front. But it did seem to him that the one-armed man lay in front.

It was still early morning and the sky was clear and cloudless. Vapor rose from the water as it had every morning up till then. The sun climbed upwards, slowly and relentlessly, and the one-armed man was dead, and the other man did not properly appreciate it yet. And perhaps the one-armed man didn't either? The things one thinks, thought the other man. Who actually knows anything at all?

[28]

The other man drank his morning shot more as a matter of habit and less because he was thirsty. He wasn't thirsty. The dead man was still fresh and, strangely enough, the other man was not thirsty. That was surely because the night had been cool.

The one-armed man had finally laid his stump down. It was no longer sticking up. For the last few days, the other man had kept wishing that this would happen, but not of course that old one-arm should be dead. The one-armed man had not laid down the stump until he was dead. In spite of that, the other man felt relieved, although he knew that it was too late.

He looked at the dead man and remembered him. In the way one usually remembers the dead. What he had said. His movements. As late as yesterday. The fever and how he had had to hold him. The beautiful nights and their drinking together and the cigarettes. As late as yesterday. How quickly yesterday passes, he thought!

The sun climbed rapidly.

The other man waited. The one-armed man stayed dead. Nothing happened. It seemed to him as if something had to happen: he looked away from the dead man and then quickly back at him. But nothing had changed.

The sun had reached noon. And so had the one-armed man. The sun began to sink, but the one-armed man went on growing. There was no end in sight.

The other man drank half of his noon ration. He had grown more sparing with cigarettes again. He considered having a piece of chewing gum.

"Better not," he said. "It might still take a long time."

He felt his teeth with his tongue. It was a strange, rough sensation. His molars, right at the back, seemed immensely large to him, as though they were cleft.

He drank the rest of his ration. He had to be careful not to drink more. His thirst beneath the fiery sun was like a funnel in the bottle. He would have gladly avoided drinking at all. For the one-armed man was not drinking. He had still drunk yesterday. They had never drunk alone, always together. He was completely aware that the one-armed man was dead. But when he drank alone, he had a bad conscience.

The one-armed man's lower lip had suddenly slipped down. The other man had not seen how it had fallen. When he had just finished drinking and looked over at the one-armed man again, his lower lip had fallen.

"Well," said the other man and slid over to him. "Excuse me." And he tried to pull the dead man's lower lip up again. But it wouldn't stay over his teeth and kept falling down. It looked as if the one-armed man were grinning.

The other man had grown scared. For when he had touched the dead man's face, it was cold. Colder than it had a right to be under this sun. He felt the dead man's legs and his arm. They were cold too. He put his hot hand on the dead man's forehead. But it did no good, his forehead stayed cold. It was clear to the touch that his forehead was not only superficially cold. His forehead had a core of ice that kept coming up and keeping it cold.

The other man quickly took his hand away and sat back down. He examined the horizon slowly and carefully. But there was nothing to be made out.

For a long time he tried not to look at the dead man. It took an effort not to look. Because there was so little there for anyone to look at.

The one-armed man grew ever more alien to him. He did not know why. For he had not changed. He was no longer the one-armed man of yesterday. Now he was a dead man.

When he finally looked at him again, he got a shock, for now the dead man was laughing straight at him. The other man screwed up his eyes, so as to see better, as if the dead man were far away. But he was still laughing. His upper lip had grown stiff in the sun and curled upwards. His lower lip hanging down and so his teeth were bared and his mouth laughing.

The other man's thoughts floated off and his heart was beating fast. The dead man began to do something. He moved. There was something behind the dead man that moved for him and was moved by him. Someone was pulling the puppet's strings.

His thoughts began to race.

This fellow, the man without an arm, and what part did the arm play? None. And aren't his legs in a different position again? His head looks like a skull without any flesh. But of course there is still flesh on it, though that laugh makes it seem like a skull and the bone is sticking out of the stump. In nature study, or was it biology, damn it, in tenth grade they had studied the human skeleton and it had been a real skeleton, probably a murderer's who had been executed, but it hadn't bothered the teacher.

For he was a joker, and the students liked him a lot. He always took off his jacket and taught in his shirtsleeves.

"The boys are now fetching our charming skeleton," he would say, and then thought over his perennial jokes. He explained the bone structure and counted the bones. He had the students feel the bones on their own bodies as far as possible. He snapped his braces with his thumbs and laughed and pointed and gave explanations.

In the next lesson, we studied the insides and outsides of the human body; the skeleton was dressed, as he put it. Ha-ha! What was important here were the sexual organs and everything connected with them. Thus we learned the purpose of the testicles, the function of the ovaries and everything connected with them. The students paid excellent attention and did not learn what they would really need later on, that was what was lacking in this joker of a teacher's instruction. He should have taught them enough for them to manage an average whore later on. Or perhaps they already could, for they were gradually approaching that age. It was the top boy, of all people, who promptly caught something. But of course the teacher could do nothing about that, neither could his parents; they hadn't said anything at all. Hoffmann's father had then quietly cleared things up for the boy, that was his specialty; it was a good thing that Hoffmann Jr. was in the class.

Later on, they quickly forgot the individual bones of the skeleton, what was the use of them anyway? But, of course, the students did not forget the other things.

But the one-armed man did not bother about how he looked. He had already begun to smell. It happens quickly in the heat. The dead man became ever more alien to the other man. At first, he smelled like hard washing soap, then like 4711 cologne, a little bit off, and then, the later it got, sweet. The other man sat at the furthest end of the dinghy and considered what was to be done.

The one-armed man's face decayed quickly. His teeth were so noticeable that the other man had to keep thinking about that damn lesson. But the dead man helped him to pass the time. He could also talk with him. He didn't dare to throw him overboard; he was afraid of being alone.

He looked at the dead man carefully and tried to think life back into the empty shape.

He doesn't look so bad after all, he said to himself. I really did like him a lot. You can't simply throw a friend into the water, like, off you go, drown, disappear, just like that, can you? Yesterday he had still been able to talk about Betsy and was moving and smoking. Now he didn't move any more and Betsy was infinitely far away.

"Did she ever really exist?" he asked the one-armed man.

But the dead man just laughed and the shadows of the

setting sun lay upon his face. His face changed as the light changed, it was kind and not evil. The other man tried to imagine what sort of face Betsy had at that moment. If one were to hold her face next to his . . . ah well, better not. I can see exactly what she looks like. Legs, higher up, wonderful teeth, and the rest. But I don't know her face. You have to be careful with faces. They are often quite different. Even faces that you've known for a long time. Like the one-armed man's.

"You over there!" he said to him. "For more than two days now I haven't seen anything but the sea and your face. Now your face looks almost like water, like this water all around here. Perhaps your face already knows that it will soon be water? Betsy's face will certainly become earth one day. Women are like that. Even if they are sometimes like Betsy. Maria died on the earth. If you really think about it, isn't that right? And faces are so soon forgotten, more quickly than a picture in a photograph album. Forgotten? You can't hold on to it, it can't be held on to. Perhaps it doesn't want to be held on to. Who knows?"

The sun changed once more from yellow into a red fire and cooled off. He put his jacket on and waited for the sun to disappear beneath the horizon; only then would he drink his evening shot of whiskey. He was very thirsty. When he thought about how thirsty he was, he had to swallow. But there was no saliva in his mouth.

The western sky had blown up into a huge explosive cloud. In the east, the cumuli that came up every evening were creeping, dark blue, over the horizon. The sky high up above him was a mixture of green and blue, very light and delicate. The first stars appeared in little clusters like pinholes. The water grew darker and looked even deeper. There was nothing in sight.

The stars soon became clearer and the other man looked for

the constellations that he knew. He slid down a little deeper and laid his neck on the rubber padding at the side; this way he could see comfortably and without getting a crick in his neck. He looked straight up at the sky. He needed only to turn and tuck in his chin to see the horizon. The plane would certainly not come searching during the night, he thought, and a U-boat's shadow could not be made out in this nocturnal light, that is unless it were coming directly at him. But that was unlikely.

Nevertheless, he sat up straight again. He had forgotten his evening shot. That's how beautiful the stars were.

He brought out the bottle and poured a shot. He had to be very careful not to pour too much into the cup. And then he drank, very slowly and in little sips. It did him good. In between, he kept looking up at the stars. He would almost have forgotten the one-armed man, if it hadn't been for the smell. But the smell was no longer so very penetrating. Perhaps he had already grown used to it. Or else the coolness of the night lessened it a little?

When he'd finished the drink, he smoked another cigarette, lay down again, and followed the outlines of the constellations.

"What is a seaman without stars?" he asked himself out loud.

"Nothing at all," he answered himself.

"You airmen don't need the stars as much as we on the sea do," he said to the one-armed man. "No wonder you don't know them. Yes, and the people on land don't need them at all. At the back there, the three weaker stars, they must be the head of the Greater Dog; Sirius should also be over the horizon at any moment. Look out for it, it looks like a steamer's masthead light. The Hare must be a bit more to starboard, there, you can see it!"

The one-armed man did not answer. But it looked as if he were also observing the sky with great care.

"New moon," said the other man. "Good light for observing. Shame we can't see the Pleiades. They are my special friends. Seven little chicks. Have you ever held little chicks in your hand? That's when you really notice what's happening. What a feeling! A woman is nothing in comparison." The other man was unexpectedly surprised that he was talking aloud. When he stopped talking aloud the silence was twice as great. He held his breath. The silence became even greater. He could hear only the noises of his own body. The pounding in his temples, the tiny clicks of his eyelids, and the waterfall in his ears: the roaring issued from the silence. When he could hold his breath no longer, he could hear his breast rising and falling and the way it echoed off his back.

He started talking again, quickly. Not as loud as before. And he told the one-armed man everything that he knew about the stars.

While he was talking he fell asleep.

With the naked eye, an observer at the equator can see about five thousand stars of magnitudes 1 through 6. If you add the telescopic stars to these, you arrive at extraordinarily high numbers of stars which, in part, can no longer be counted, and we are left to rely on estimates (as, for example, in the case of stellar fogs and clouds).

In order to obtain a better overview, the large stars have been grouped into constellations that are named after heroes, animals, and the most diverse objects. Individual, very bright stars have, in addition, been given special names.

The significance that the stars, even fixed stars and also planets, have for human beings is manifold. The mystic view of astrology and the exact science of astronomy are formally separate, but in the intellectual history of mankind they have from time immemorial formed a peculiar combination which, even today, leads to the strangest results.

The other man slept fitfully.

He would often rise up, look absent-mindedly around the horizon, lie down again, and go back to sleep.

Towards morning, he slept more lightly and started to dream. Strangely enough, he was completely aware that he was dreaming.

I must write that down at once, he said to himself. As I used to, with pencil and paper on the night table. Maria liked to busy herself with dreams, and I enjoy it too. It's like being on a swing. You go head over heels and Maria shouts with glee. How quickly the boat turns; it turns like a funnel, becoming narrower and narrower, becoming faster and deeper, becoming, becoming, becoming . . . Gerundive form. A gerundive funnel. Who has ever seen a four-sided gerundive? Nobody answers? Good, one up to the one-armed man. But what's the dead man's pipe doing? It's pointing straight at me. Since when has he been smoking a pipe? That's not done, pointing at people. And Maria is laughing. That's not at all funny. You see, that's what comes of it, and now the faces are pouring into the funnel and disappearing at the distant, bottomless point. But there, it's coming up again, it's turning around and coming up again. But it's not turning any more, it's spreading out, it's the sea, and the water is trickling over me. Listen!

He was lying down below on the seabed and above him shone the green crystal of the surface. Ships came sailing along there. Columbus, the bloody fool, shouted out something. What did he shout? Nothing you could understand. The distance is too great. Betsy climbs out of the great big ship with the gaudy sails and climbs down its ladder to him. He can see under her skirts because she climbs down so vulgarly, she clearly wants to climb down like that. What else does she want, I wonder? She turns around and he cannot recognize her face. There is frosted glass in front of it.

[36]

"Give me the arm that was taken off," she says, but where is he going get it so quickly? She makes a short, sweet moue and then swims away like a jellyfish, her tentacles gently bent down into the depths. He can't run very fast in the silt down here; he would have liked very much to chat with her for a bit, because he is so lonely and because he is afraid. Because it is growing dark and he can see nothing more.

When it had grown completely black he felt himself seized by a hand and lifted up. The water ran off him and his skin was freezing cold again.

Now it's light again and the gigantic face of the doctor-airman is close in front of him, hacked to pieces and craggy like a rock.

"There you are at last," said the dead man. "Why didn't you come earlier? I've got to operate now."

Behind his shoulder, the nature study teacher is sharpening the great knife. The grindstone squeals and sparks fly from it. More and more sparks are thrown up, a firework display with rockets and sparklers. The faces disappear in the flaming stars and sparkling, dripping letters are formed out of the Catherine wheels.

They say, "In case of danger, pull the emergency brake."

Where is the emergency brake? He looks and looks. "No emergency brake," he wants to shout, but he cannot cry out. The moon has grown larger. Then the writing explodes with a great bang and Maria's lips are on his mouth and everything is all right. Immediately afterwards there is another explosion and he protects himself against the debris that is raining down from above. And there is the airplane, a fat four-engine plane rushes towards him. It is burning. But apparently the airmen are not bothered by the fact that they are being turned into coke up there. He cowers in front of the monster that is storming towards him, he sees in the mirror that it is a cockroach, flat and stupid. But in spite of that he cannot run and the airplane keeps coming closer. The bomb doors yawn open and now the giant bomb falls. The pilot up there has gone crazy, he's pushing the crate down, he's going to ram us, the swine, with the burning airplane. And where are the other cockroaches? The bomb, the bomb . . . then immediately it explodes.

A dream is defined as conscious events during sleep. The ear, the nose, and the sense of touch all remain subject to external influences during sleep and influence ideas during a dream. The content of dreams consists mainly of the revival and combination of images from memory. Self-consciousness is not entirely suspended, rather it begins to stir, especially towards morning, often in the form of doubts and in the form of a question of whether one is really dreaming.

But it didn't go bang.

It was simply that his head had fallen down and lay on the bottom of the dinghy as he woke up.

"I was dreaming," he said, and quickly removed his left leg from the dead man's feet. Where did Maria go when the aircraft came, and the cockroaches? The pilot must either have been crazy or had been burned to death to ram us with the burning machine. Sheer suicide. The one-armed man lay unchanged. The other man had a headache and shut his eyes.

Everything was not all right.

He breathed deeply a few times and spat. But nothing came out of his mouth. He had to cough. His mouth tasted as though he had been drinking all night. Or after coitus, if the movie was broken.

"Never again," he had said, then, "damned crap," and now you were dreaming about it.

Already he was not completely sure what he had dreamed about. Only the taste in his mouth was still there. He chewed a piece of gum. The furry taste wouldn't go away.

He turned up the collar of his jacket. He was freezing cold.

[38]

In the east, a narrow streak of light burst into flame above the horizon. The morning was approaching. The sea lay like a board. The stars quickly grew pale.

He was freezing cold. His skin was damp from the coolness of the night. He put his hands in the water. The water was frighteningly warm and reminded him of the coming day. There was not the tiniest movement around his hands in the water. The dinghy was stuck as though it were nailed to the spot. It was not moving anywhere.

"Not anywhere? That's a good direction."

He took his hands out of the water again quickly, as quickly as if a snake had bitten him. He dried his hands on his shirt. They began to grow freezing cold in the air. He knew the feeling. He hated it.

"Not in any direction, now at last I know!" he said again. "And you?" he asked the dead man. "Not going anywhere either? That's what's called 'progress.' Or perhaps you've arrived already? How can you get anywhere if you are not going anywhere?"

The dead man did not answer, as usual. This not-answering embittered the other man. He knew it was stupid to wait for an answer. He knew that it was idiotic to want to talk to a dead man. He knew that his thoughts were dangerous. He knew everything with absolute precision. But he couldn't do anything else. It was a fascination. He had to talk. Say things which, at the very moment he said them, he knew he should not, so that he wouldn't go out of his mind. He was angry with the one-armed man again and still mad at himself because of it; behind it all was just the craving to challenge an answer from the one who was pulling the strings in the background and who had arranged the whole thing.

"Arranged!" he shouted. "What a wonderfully appropriate word."

"When I say that, I don't mean the God you read of in

schoolbooks, my friend!" he said to the one-armed man, more softly and gently this time. "God is much too harmless in those. I know what you would say, old pal, if you weren't done for. Thinker-plus-poet's grandchild, western culture digs for the philosopher's stone. Eh? That's what you would say. Wouldn't you?"

In spite of all that, we're going nowhere, he thought. I am alive and you are dead and together we are both going nowhere, there's no difference. It's just that I am alone and you perhaps are not. You are dead and have it all behind you, I am still alive. Anyway, you are at least dead.

"That is no small advantage," he said to the one-armed man. "A noble way of putting it, what do you think?"

He hadn't been freezing cold for a long time now. The sun burned down just as it had on the previous days. He took his jacket off and immediately felt as if someone were pouring hot water into all his pores. The heat penetrated him like fine sheets of flame. He had difficulty speaking precisely and articulately. The sounds staggered about in his mouth. There had been no nocturnal coolness.

He tried to speak clearly.

"La-le-lo-lu-len-til," he said, and his tongue got stuck everywhere, "Cre-creep. Cham-pagne break-fast," he articulated. But it didn't work. Everything was bone dry. He gave up speaking. Thirst enveloped his whole body, that was how it felt. The other man breathed through his nose, so that his mouth was not completely dried out by the flickering air. But what good was it?

None at all.

He took out the bottle. There were at most three rations left. For a day—for two days, if you cut the rations in two.

In two, that's too little, he figured. I can't cut myself in two. So better to have a full ration and then tomorrow it'll all be over. All right. They're not going to find me, in any case. One day longer, what difference does that make at this point? Better to go down with all flags flying.

"Heroism, my dear friend! Just as it is in the pictures of heroes or in the movies or in the national schoolbooks!"

But when he looked at the one-armed man, he drank only half a ration. He counted the pieces of chewing gum. There were still four precious little white pieces there. The Chocacola box was empty. He still had eight cigarettes and two-thirds of a butt. He was smoking that now.

"Everything is just growing less," he said.

"You too!" he shouted at the one-armed man. "You too, if you look at it that way."

The one-armed man was no longer the one-armed man at all. The one-armed man was now a completely red something. There was scarcely any resemblance to his dead friend. "No similarity," he said aloud and as clearly as he could. He sucked the smoke in and the liquor turned over in his stomach. His head was reeling and the horizon was moving gently.

Hold tight, he told himself, you mustn't go crazy now. Otherwise it's all over. Just think it over nice and quietly. The dead man has got to go. I can't put up with the smell and the sight any longer.

He looked over at the dead man. The stump of his arm was almost perpendicular to his body.

The other man closed his eyes and then looked over at him again. The stump of his arm was almost perpendicular to his body. It was not an illusion. The dead man's stomach was a little swollen and his eyes were partly open. There was a gleam of white from the slits of his eyes. The dead man's underside was damp through.

"To hell with it," said the other man.

He looked away again. He could no longer look at what had been his neighbor. It was no use, it was too much for him. And God knows he had seen enough dead people, completely, half-

[41]

rotted, freshly drowned, and after they had been in the water for months. But this one here, the remains of the one-armed man, was too much. There was nothing more to be done. He was no longer the one-armed man of the previous days. Now he was his enemy. Someone who was out to get him. Someone who was attacking him. Someone who was doing something, although he was dead and could not do anything. And the other man remembered earlier times. Just being able to remember was good for him. In this way he knew that he could still think clearly. He remembered what he had once thought about dead people. The dead man decomposing here was a confirmation of his thoughts.

His mind was completely clear and sharp as a scalpel. That was good.

"That's good!" he said, and was pleased with the clear construction of the sentences in which he was thinking. What had he just been thinking? Repeat it once again.

"A romanticism that is aimed at the past can easily be cynical with relation to the present," he said. "All right, my brain's functioning. That at least is an advantage. Thank you, my friend," he said to the one-armed man. "The dead Maria and the living Maria: that is a huge difference! You have to draw a strict line between the two. Otherwise, you're finished, pal!" He opened his eyes again.

The dead man had not changed.

The alcohol raged in his blood. "You have a complex," he said to himself. "A death complex. You can't go on like this!" He frowned so that he could go on thinking precisely and consequentially. In earlier days, he had always done that if he had been dead drunk, just so that he could think properly.

"The dead man has to go," he said. He spoke loud enough for the dead man to hear him.

Yet the dead man said nothing. What else was he to do?

Dead people never say anything. Dead people speak only through their presence in the feelings of others.

The other man suddenly exploded:

"I don't want you! Not you and not Maria or tomorrow and not myself either! When you're dead, it's all over! Finis! End!"

The other man scarcely knew what he was shouting any more and grew afraid of the one-armed man, and beneath the other man there was something somewhere, deep in the water, an animal that was gaping at him from down below, an octopus, wondering what that could be up there, that dark spot on the surface. The other man felt that it was watching him. Perhaps it was a giant fish with sharp teeth that were waiting for him, waiting to eat him up when he was in the water and about to sink, or perhaps it was enough just to push upwards, or perhaps just a piece of carrion would suffice, he thought, get rid of the dead man. Then the dead man will be gone, in the belly of a fish or in the octopus's sack, then I will finally be on my own. And what then?

The other man was almost weeping from sheer horror and relief. He had to throw the one-armed man overboard, that much was clear. The great octopus was waiting underneath for food. Get rid of the dead man. Get rid of all dead men. Throw him overboard. That thing down there wants to eat, so eat it will.

The depths, the eye below, were turning around in the other man's head, and his thoughts went awry.

The voice whispered.

"You two, you'll not be found and you will be sailing through eternity with the dead man. The sun will melt you to pieces and you will merge and become one and the sun will fuse you together. Your flesh will melt away and your bones will become polished white and brittle with the heat, two skeletons in an embrace, for you belong together. Forever and ever. Ever."

"Quiet!" shouted the other man. "Quiet!"

His heartbeats pounded in his ears. He pulled himself together with difficulty, and after a small pause while he took a quick breath, the crazy merry-go-round disappeared just as quickly as it had come. He could now see clearly again and knew plainly that he was here and the dead man was there. The mid-Atlantic was all around, the tropical sun was above him, and there was seventy-five hundred feet of water below him. The stars were invisibly high in the sky.

"There's a lot there that cannot be seen, d'you see?" he said to the one-armed man.

He moved over to him and got him ready. He looked to see whether there would be anything left of him, whether there was still anything in the dead man's jacket.

He found his wallet in his jacket and an empty cigarette case, flat, elegant, and engraved with the name "Betsy." There was a handkerchief, matches, and a nail file in his pants pocket. The other man laughed and sobbed:

"Nail file—what a lot of things a nail file is good for!" In his other pants pocket there was a broken stump of a pencil. Someone had been unable to write any more because the pencil was broken. In addition, there was a piece of ribbon and a cardboard packet. He opened the packet and looked in it. He was disgusted and threw it overboard.

"That wasn't necessary, you swine!" he said.

"Bloody swine!" he shouted and would have liked to hit him. He felt his thoughts floating away again and could hear himself sobbing.

"You too, Betsy!" he screamed.

But Betsy was not there, so he could go on shouting for a long time. He calmed himself down again because no one was there. Why Betsy too? Wasn't it always too . . .

He broke off. What am I thinking about, he thought. That's how the sublime gravity of death goes down the drain, he thought derisively. That's how it should be. Bravo! That's also something for the creator of all things. The chief rubber maker becomes ridiculous in the face of his own product, ha-ha.

The other man shook with laughter.

"Creation stops in the face of a little piece of rubber," he declaimed. "If it doesn't want it to happen, there's nothing he can do about it!"

And he remembered La Gracieuse, the little mademoiselle, and forgot the other thing completely. She had been really charming, God knows.

A few months ago down in Bordeaux they had had a meal in the Central, the food was wonderful, and afterwards they had gone to the Cotelette Bar, a nasty place, but what the hell. Of course, after that he had gone home with her, and why not, why shouldn't he go home with a cute young girl? Such a graceful young thing. A slender creature, he recalled.

It had been a bit more than usual. The little thing had been in love with him, a blind man could see that. She was charming and saw to it that he didn't drink too much, a good sign. When they got home, as she was undressing, she told him about her life. Her life had certainly not been easy, the war and everything else. She had a wonderful figure and he had sat in the armchair smoking and watching the whole performance. When she noticed, she began to cry. She wasn't used to that. And she was still sobbing when they were in bed, and they had just lain there side by side. He looked up at the ceiling of the room and a car went by outside, the lights played on the ceiling. She was sobbing and he was thinking.

Until she started making her damn little movements, in spite of her sobbing, and then, of course, there was no more thinking, what can a fellow do? She was no longer sobbing and he was no longer thinking, her mouth was a little wet animal and he let himself fall, where did they let themselves fall to, and the passion mounted and the flame and the fire exuded heat, there was no more light on the ceiling and no ceiling either, little La Gracieuse.

He had thrown the cardboard packet overboard and his anger at the one-armed man had passed. What did he know about him, anyway? Was Betsy like La Gracieuse? Perhaps, but then perhaps not. Almost certainly not, in spite of her Florida father. Girls like that are sometimes unexpectedly modest. What do I know about the one-armed man's graceful girl? All right! A good thing that the packet's gone, he thought.

"That rubbish is illusory now as far as you're concerned!" he said to the one-armed man and buttoned up his jacket. It was tight over his distended stomach. He went on talking to the dead man.

"You don't need that any more. I've thrown it away. The fish can amuse themselves with it now. You don't need that rubbish for Betsy or for anyone else now. I'm sorry to call it that, but we are alone, aren't we? Decent people with morals also go at it hard but they don't talk about it; well, let them. But perhaps you forgot it once and there's a son of yours living somewhere? That would be nice for you. A son of your La Gracieuse, do you think she's happy about it? Perhaps she isn't. Be glad that you have a son, my friend. Most girls of that sort only play and then paint a fresh mouth on themselves, and that's all. And then that's our bad luck. Oh! Leave it. Come on, be quiet. My La Gracieuse? Don't talk about her. And leave Maria alone, I tell you!

The other man grew louder again.

"You and your damned cardboard packet have no right to talk about it. You least of all!"

The sun stood exactly at noon.

The other man looked at his watch. The watch had stopped.

In a sudden burst of rage he threw the watch far out into the water.

"Time is sinking," he said, when he was able to think again. "Ah well, what does it matter?"

And then he lifted the one-armed man up and rolled him over the rubber padding on the dinghy's side. He gave him a shove and turned around so as not to follow the dead man with his eyes.

The dinghy was rocked a little by the sudden shock. Flat, sluggish circles undulated from it towards the horizon. But otherwise the sea was dead calm. In the distance there was the whirr of a flock of flying fish. Otherwise there was nothing in sight.

The other man lay down on the bottom of the dinghy and turned his face towards the corner, but it was not dark enough there. He pulled his jacket over his head: now it was dark enough. Then he wept.

3

Thirst (Lat. *sitis*) is the unpleasant feeling in the mucous membrane at the back of the throat and the oral cavity, by which the body's need for liquid is made apparent. Thirst arises from substantial perspiration after sustained muscular activity, when there is considerable dryness or high air temperatures, as well as after the consumption of highly salted food. Thirst can be quenched by drinking water; in certain cases water can be administered by subcutaneous injection.

If thirst is not quenched, the oral mucous membrane reddens, speech becomes hoarse, and swallowing is difficult. All bodily secretions are reduced. A general physical weakness and an increased irritability of the nervous system are also present. The oral mucous membrane and the throat then become inflamed. The pulse becomes extremely rapid, breathing is accelerated and labored. High fever and delirious speech, as well as unconsciousness, follow. Unconsciousness finally terminates in death.

The other man had pulled his jacket over his head and his face was covered in darkness.

He could not stand anything around him. He was scared of the empty place where the one-armed man had been lying. His head lay in darkness and his jacket had also formed a solid wall around him. Yet the jacket pressed down on him like a heavy weight. He felt everything in his body with an enormous clarity, just as if his skin were immeasurably expanded. Every single touch of his shirt felt rough and painful. The watch missing from his left wrist was there in the reversal of its absence, its not-being-there also hurt.

"I've no time," he said.

His thinking was like his skin, sensitive and unusually clear.

"I've no time. It has disappeared in the water over there." His weeping abated. His eyes were so unbearably painful that he became angry again.

"Time thrown away, and nothing in exchange!" he said more loudly. "That's not much of a deal."

He now simply had to smoke a cigarette. He looked for the pack in his pants pocket. But it wasn't there. He had to sit up and take his jacket off. The heat and the light struck him like a grenade. He opened his mouth wide and gulped down some air. His mouth was filled with a glowing, swelling mass.

He finally found the cigarettes.

While he was smoking, he kept his eyes fixed on the inside of the dinghy. He tried to take his mind off the one-armed man and did not dare to look at the surrounding water. The cigarette smoke tasted bitter in his mouth and swept, burning, over his dry tongue. He exerted his whole will to get away from the dead man and concentrated on his missing watch and the time he was missing.

"Philosophical thought is what matters," he said, speaking out loud again. He had to speak out loud. There was no other way.

"Methodical thought. Otherwise we reach no conclusions," he said, and the effort really made him almost forget the dead man.

"What is it about time?" he asked. "Well, Mr. Einstein? Curved space? Curved time? Curved human being?"

He laughed.

"Curved human being is good," he shouted. "Excellent. Now there's a thought!"

He snapped his fingers. He was amused by his civilized thoughts.

Well? What is it? he thought. Curved space? Good. Curved time? More difficult. We'll get to curved human being in time. Please, sir, that experiment hasn't been completed yet. Please think very carefully. What was it? At the time there was endless discussion about it.

It was back before the war had begun. There was a so-called circle of clever people in the town. They visited one another's houses and took an active part in the cultural life. And so on. Of course, artists belonged to the circle. And doctors as well, of course. They are present always and everywhere, the one-armed man would have said.

Actually, it was always very nice. The people were clever, as I said, and made an effort to get to the bottom of things. Discussing life's problems. A lot of good things were drunk during those evenings, whatever you felt like. A good late vintage, or a mixed rum and porter, fifty-fifty, wonderful.

He could recall one particular evening when they were discussing "curved time" and so on. Curved people were then not so obviously existent—at least not as far as the circle was concerned. It had been a difficult discussion and finally came down to the same old story, the banal question of the famous "meaning." The female speakers laid bare their complexes, of course, and the male speakers explained what they would nevertheless never achieve. And they were all afraid. Years later, one could see that.

The other man grinned at the memory. He had already known it at the time: the declaration of longing. For that's what these many words really were. He had known it at the time, in any case, his own self-respect had been correspondingly inflated. Of course he hadn't said so to the others, people don't respond well to their own stasis.

"Nor do you!" the other man said out loud to himself.

But there was one thing that he had not known at the time: that basically it was quite simple. Did he know now?

"All right then, fire away with your sayings," he said, and basked in the sunshine. "And formulate them well, if you don't mind!" The other man pondered, struck a pose and was highly delighted with his wisdom.

"What is simple?" he said. "On the outside, everyone has to do what he has been charged to do. No talking and questioning, but doing. And on the inside? There, there is only one way, the way towards yourself, the movement towards yourself. To fill your own limits to the greatest possible extent."

That might be a bit too much Rilke, the other man thought. He kept on talking.

"Looked at in this way, there is no great 'You' in the plural. Progress does not rest in the plural but in the most extreme singular. But of course no public person wants to admit the truth of that."

He paused, felt pleased, and laughed.

"I did express myself in a very educated way, didn't I?" He pursed his lips and repeated "eduuucated." The word sounded silly as he said it to the water all around him. He went on thinking:

What really came out of that curved evening? Everything had been wonderfully defined. People knew more than they had before. Did it help? In a certain way. Yes. The perspectives had become larger. But otherwise?

"But I'm dying of thirst here!" he said, louder this time, and the fun had gone out of him. "That's a cheerful way to get to myself. A way where there is nothing at all left over!"

He had remembered his thirst again and such lucid remnants of thought as he still had immediately evaporated. Everything was mixed up, the people back then and he himself, here and now. What he really meant, and the twisted pieces of wisdom. It was impossible for him to make up his mind as to what he already felt and what he still did not know.

"Good God!" he said, and did not mean him at all.

He lay down again and pulled his jacket over his head. This way, it was dark again and he could leave what he did not want outside in the light.

He didn't weep now either. There was simply nothing more there, and he was no longer thinking. He listened to the thirst in his body. The hiss of his breath was loud in the darkness that surrounded his head.

It was only towards evening that he emerged from this semi-wakeful state. He did not know whether he had been asleep. He just felt tuckered out. The heavy weights were once more pressing on his movements.

He turned over so that he was lying on his back looking up into the burning sky.

So no one came today either, he thought. He found it hard to think and it took a lot out of him. In fact, everything took a lot out of him: thinking about something specific, raising his hand, moving his foot.

No aircraft and no ship had come, he thought. Nothing has come. How long have I been on this damned rubber dinghy anyway?

"Not easy, calculating!" he said out loud again, and gave up trying to calculate the exact number of days. What were days, nights, hours, or weeks in these circumstances, anyway? Nothing. Or everything! In any case, not things that could be measured. Was there any sense in still having hope? Who was looking for him? No one. The aircraft were looking for the one-armed man and his people, who had already been dead long since. The aircraft were still only looking for the dead. That is, if they were looking at all! He, the other man, would not yet be missed at home. How should the people at home know what had happened in the meantime? That they should go out and look for him? The U-boats would often go for weeks without sending any radio messages. Oh, well. He wouldn't be missed. And who else should have been in the picture? The authorities, of course. And beyond that? Maria was dead.

"One nil for Mr. Thanatos," he said.

His parents had died when he was still a child. Two nil for Death. And what else?

"That fellow is gradually gaining ground," he said. "The one-armed man is another trump card in his hand. Trumps take the trick, my friend! What can you pit against them?" he asked.

"Nothing," he answered.

He realized that he was talking out loud again. What nonsense, since no one was listening to him.

"I must think about something else," he said to himself. "Otherwise it will turn into a compulsive complex, a thought-circus from which I will not get out again. You can only afford cheap comforting philosophy when you're at home by the fireside. It's out of place here. Otherwise the story becomes deadly."

He sat up and looked at the horizon. The west was a sea of fire in the setting sun.

"If someone were to paint that, it would be a magnificent piece of kitsch," he said. "Those candy colors!" And then he laughed. "So you couldn't find a better general sentiment, eh?"

The west was dazzling in the sunset and in the east all the dark colors of the night were indistinguishably merged. The horizon could only be made out in places. He thought of the one-armed man. He took the wallet out and inspected its contents.

[53]

There was the dead man's identity card. With a stamp and a signature. A well-worn piece of paper.

"I wouldn't have recognized you again," he said. "An idiotic picture. What do you identify yourself as with a thing like that?" he asked. "You don't need an identity card any longer now. That's to say, you never know, perhaps you have to show the people over there an identity card, so that they can sort you out in an orderly fashion." Then there was a receipt for $7.60. The writing was so unclear that he couldn't make out what the one-armed man had bought. Pity.

There were a few stamps in one of the little side pockets. Colorful little pieces of paper printed with Mr. Washington's face.

"For five cents each," he said. "Faces have become that cheap. Aha! A movie ticket, another movie ticket," he went on, "holding hands and a happy end. Madly exciting. True to life, wonderful."

The other man was again amused and grew warm at the thought of the movies.

"Gripping psychological drama and a hundred thousand bare legs. The famous star's upward glance. The seriatim abdomens of the revue girls. The mind's a butcher shop and the body's an abattoir. No more slogans?"

Nothing else came to him. Only the faces of the audience afterwards, he could still remember them as though he were looking at them at that moment: the bloated faces swollen with the heat and the phony dreams presented to them. And the way the people went home afterwards, a nervous cigarette in their mouths and embittered about their petty grey lives, which were nothing like what they had seen on the screen.

He quickly tried to think of something else and went on looking in the wallet. At the back, in the big compartment, there was a letter from Betsy and a picture of her.

He looked carefully at Betsy's picture. It was a well-lit

photograph only slightly retouched. A pretty face, no doubt about it. Very large eyes, her hair a wreath of rays of light around her head. The mouth not too large and not too small. The nose a little retroussé, a cute little nose. "Everything's right in that face," the other man said. "It's even better than I thought. If the photographer hadn't done such a competent job, there would be more to see." He buried himself more deeply in the face. A strange face. He did not know it and yet he knew a lot about it. Fräulein Betsy. Miss Betsy.

"A pity you can't talk," he said, "I would have liked to talk to you. And seen your face from all sides. Not as it is here. You will excuse me if I read your letter? The one-armed man is dead, I'm not taking anything away from him, am I?"

But he didn't read the letter yet. Because Betsy's face began to disappear and another face came up behind the one that had grown unclear. Maria came back.

The first thing of Maria's that he had seen was her picture. It was standing on his sister's desk one day. And then at some point, as it turned out, they had visited Maria on their way to I've forgotten where. When they got out of the train, Maria was already there and waiting for them. At first he had had a shock, for Maria looked quite different from her picture. But the shock soon passed.

The two girls started talking to each other immediately, and he stood by stupidly. They were talking like a waterfall. Good heavens, what girls always have to talk about! Back at home, in her room, they had coffee and the girls went on talking. He had sat there listening and looking at Maria when she wasn't looking.

That evening after dinner they drank a white Bordeaux: he could still remember exactly what it had tasted like. Maria was as lively as a cricket, my God, and the girls talked and talked and talked. Maria was swinging her legs, she seemed

[55]

very happy. Later on, they began to get a bit silly, for when they got hungry again, very late in the evening, Maria cooked her Sunday roast, that's to say they were cutlets, and he had had to chop the meat up first. A man's work, my friend, how silly can you get? He'd chopped the meat up with a hatchet out front on the stone steps leading to the front door, and whatever did the neighbors think!

He had no choice in the matter, he had fallen in love with Maria. And as for Maria? The gods alone knew about her. They drank more wine and now he spoke a little too. They conversed brilliantly. Later on, he had grown tired and the girls talked on their own again. He had fallen into a suspended, unreal state. The only thing that was real was Maria's face, as it moved when she spoke, as her thoughts crossed it. Her mouth had a very characteristic line down below under her lower lip. And her mouth was very red. Don't keep looking, my friend! And her hair in the lamp light . . . She had put a veil over her hair and was explaining something to his sister from a play in which the veil played a special part. What was she saying? Oh right, Hofmannsthal. *Death and the Fool,* The Beloved.

"Were you in it?" he asked.

Yes, she had played The Beloved.

"Where, here?"

"Yes, here."

"The play's a bit sentimental," he'd said.

"A play for those who have missed out on something, eh? Suffering is trumps." he'd said. Although he knew it was nonsense. And Maria had grown angry because she liked Hofmannsthal, that's what he really wanted to know.

"It was lovely," she quoted, "and you are to blame for . . ."

All right, that's enough.

Strange, how little he had understood at the time.

And then the girls went on talking and talking.

He sat silent, looking at Maria, and the place where she lived. He already knew it all by heart, after only a few hours. It was indescribably beautiful, simply sitting there in the corner and looking at everything. How often, later on, had he sat in the corner of her room, in good times and bad.

But now he was sitting alone in the rubber dinghy and it was too late.

Too late, he thought. Too late for Maria? Maria is dead. Too late for me? I'm still alive. Too late for the bad times, of course. And what now?

"I'm still alive," he said and breathed deeply a few times. Did he still have a little time left? Here on this lonely rubber dinghy?

It had grown dark again. The stars were not shining as brightly as on the previous nights. A light veil of mist lay in front of them in the sky and made their light more subdued and not so cold.

He put Betsy's picture back into the wallet and did not read her letter. It was no use, it wasn't right to read the letter. Because of the one-armed man and also so as not to get too close to Betsy. Besides which it had grown too dark. He lay on his back and looked up into the night sky again. He felt himself growing sentimental.

A person looks up at the sky and becomes emotional, he thought and he escaped to the place where he thought he was safe. It's all because of the thoughts of Maria, he thought. It comes from my inferiority complex vis-à-vis the stars. According to the maxim: I am so small and you are so infinitely far away, I am so tiny and the universe is so large. The "breath" of the universe, the awe in the face of infinity, the god behind the Milky Way, the little human being, the insignificant one alone in the face of all that.

He laughed. He was enjoying himself again.

"Little Luise Miller thoughts," he said out loud again. "A reminder of the philosophers of all the ages and nothing else!"

He spoke louder and louder.

"They simply rewrite it in different words and think about it more consistently and write what they don't know with a lot of foreign words. Homo singularis vis-à-vis the great unknown. Oh, well. It's always the same. Always. Endlessly repeated. Basically it's all the same."

"Everything is one!" he said more loudly. "If you speak Greek say 'eï' for it. What use is it?" he asked.

"Nothing," he answered himself, with satisfaction. "Incidentally, a cunning thought: Lieschen Miller equals Plato, Eva Meier equals Confucius. Emil Krause equals Goethe. Always the same. Only the form of expression is different. A function expressed mathematically. Ha-ha. Function, that's that sort of a word too . . . And only the degree of differentiation of this function determines the quality of the man?"

He became more and more cynical and he thought more and more. He knew that things were or were not in agreement and how they were or were not in agreement and he felt inspired by their varied, adjustable perspectives. And he became more angry because he was alone and could not help himself in any other way. But he didn't want to help himself in any other way or let himself be helped, he knew precisely and clearly that that was not what he wanted, for otherwise it would have been too easy, and you could guarantee that it would not help, either to live or to die.

"That can't be done any longer," he said.

And then he was frightened.

"Perhaps the only possible thing is the most primitive thing?" he asked himself.

"Perhaps the assessment and use of facts in the sense of civilization is the only possibility? Otherwise you automatically kick the bucket? Otherwise modern life, progress, is insupportable?"

"No ressentiments," he said and repeated more loudly: "No ressentiments, please! They get you nowhere."

But then what should the other lead to? He continued to ponder. I am alone and what is supposed to lead me where? Answer please!

Pause.

"Who's supposed to answer," he said, this time more softly. "Me myself perhaps? Heavens above!"

He began to laugh again.

"Speculations and thoughts: real life consists of action and deed. By their deeds shall ye know them, isn't that what it says? You can't produce a play without a plot, otherwise the theater gets boring. What interest do ideas and thoughts contain? Gentlemen, thought must be made visible, images must be invented for it, please demonstrate thought by dramatic action! Hell," he said, "it makes me sick. What's the use of all this? Here, in my case, as I am slowly but surely dying of thirst and only have a little time left? I can no longer be splendidly bothered about a plot or about dramatics in the way literary people or other people who know how to make the best of life are. There are other things that are important here and that are only valid here."

"Valid!" he cried, "Valid! Good Lord, you're alone and dying on this damned rubber dinghy, what sort of nonsense are you babbling? What's the purpose of these attempts at a construction? It is quite simple," he shouted, "it's revoltingly simple: you are dying, my dearest friend, and you want to justify yourself. So you talk, don't you? So you babble on, eh? You act as though you were in parliament and were introducing a resolution on your own death."

His thoughts grew more and more confused. He had forgotten to drink his evening ration. His thirst had entered a stage where it was present only in his subconscious, but this made it all the more dangerous. He had not even thought about the cigarettes.

He was now lying on his back and looking up at the sky and was laughing about the lack of drama and plot in the play that he was performing. In between times, he listened to what was happening in his body, how the weakness was settling into his arms and legs and was making everything difficult. He recollected a hundred thousand things about his life and he placed them, almost sensually, into a particular relationship with his present situation. It amused him to torment himself.

He remembered and nothing happened. The images passed him by, good and bad, beautiful and repellent images, but nothing came of them. The stars twinkled poetically and the sea lay picturesque and motionless and it was uncannily quiet all around and nothing happened. The horizon was completely unobscured in the light of the waning day.

Nothing happened.

The stars moved slowly across the sky in their crooked arcs, and the other man was moving imperceptibly in the Atlantic towards nothing. The moon came out and was only a narrow transparent crescent, waxing. Then, towards morning, even this little crescent grew pale and the other man did not see it any more, because he was asleep. He had fallen asleep. In spite of everything.

And he was on board his U-boat again and the radio message had just come through. The boat was now proceeding at high speed towards the convoy that had been reported.

It was the same as always, the diesels sang a descant and the boat shook with their power, the conning tower took on a lot of water and the bow sometimes heaved so heavily in the sea that you could fear it would never come up again. They were lying not far from the southern tip of Greenland and it was bitterly cold. They were up there in Anton Karl, the lousy region where there was always a lot of shooting.

It was quiet in the boat. The crew was asleep and only the men on watch on the conning tower were scanning the sky and the horizon ceaselessly through their heavy night glasses. The chief engineer, sitting in the little officers' mess, was quiet and piggish as always and was playing some passages from the Brahms violin concerto on his violin, the torpedo mate was sitting by the forward set of torpedo tubes near his "fish"; he was examining them for the hundredth time and, in the intervals, was reading his everlasting crime novel. There was nothing in his life apart from torpedoes, girls, and books.

Towards midnight they reached the convoy. It was pitch dark. The night was only occasionally lit up by a burning ship, and when that happened it was possible to get some sort of overview of the situation. So, there were other U-boats there already and they had already launched an attack. The convoy was making desperate evasive maneuvers. Some ships had already been destroyed.

The crew was at battle stations, the torpedoes ready, and in the conning tower the first officer of the watch was waiting behind the sights of the torpedo tubes. The first officer was a minister by profession but he was now a reserve officer who had volunteered for duty. According to the tenet "love your enemies." For him the war had become a sort of private revenge, for enemy bombers had not only destroyed his church and his house but had also sent his wife to everlasting salvation. He had not liked that and had become angry. Even diligent reading in the book of Job had not been of any help. Whenever he shot off a salvo of torpedoes, he always said, "Do good to all," and for every ship that was sunk he drank a good cognac and drew a beautiful cross in his Bible, at the back, on the last page. And he was completely aware of what he was doing.

But now he was looking for his target.

The boat positioned itself for firing. "Permission to fire," said the captain. But before they could shoot, the boat had to go hard about and beat it. A destroyer had seen them and was firing like mad. It came at them head on. They had to take wide evasive action and had already given up hope for the night, when in the first light of dawn they saw a giant tanker that had apparently been in a collision and was lying there without making any way, guarded by two corvettes.

They snaked their way towards it, unnoticed, and the minister shot off three linked single shots from a range of twelve hundred feet. "Do good to all," he said, "that should finish her off." The tanker blew up with the very first torpedo. It was gone. A giant explosion. It must have been carrying gasoline. They simply could not understand where the ship had gone, although they had indeed seen it. Simply disappeared in a giant fireball.

But then they had to dive quickly, because the tanker, blown into its component parts, started to fall from the sky again. They had been too close to it. If a piece were to hit their boat, they would be finished. So emergency dive. Not one of the tanker's crew had come down; it had all happened at lightning speed.

So they dived. The first officer drew a particularly beautiful cross in his New Testament and drank his usual cognac.

The boat had remained at periscope depth. In the meantime, it had grown light. The two corvettes threw a few depth charges blindly in the vicinity and then withdrew. It didn't seem to be all that important to them.

And then, just as they had loaded new torpedoes, a passenger ship hove into view in the periscope, a rag merchant, as these ships were called. The rag merchants' job was to come along behind the convoy to pick up the people who had been left in the water off the ships that had been torpedoed the previous night.

So, everyone back to battle stations. Attack.

The ship was already in their crosshairs and was down at the stern after the first torpedo struck it aft. The next torpedo struck between the bridge and the smokestack. The ship broke in two and quickly sank. There were a lot of people swimming in the water. Not a pretty sight. The sea was very rough. The people could not survive for long in the water.

When they had dived and were slowly sailing away, three destroyers suddenly appeared. They were making straight for them. The submarine dived quickly to maximum depth. "A plus 120," said the chief officer, and directed the hydroplane guests with his fiddle bow. "Now we're in for it."

In the hydrophones, they could hear the destroyers coming on relentlessly. They were paying no attention to the people in the water; instead they were attacking. They were old, experienced hands: now this could become interesting. Pick-pick, that was their direction finder, their Asdic had picked up the U-boat, and now the first Brit was making his run to fire depth charges. He was being damn accurate. "Full speed ahead both engines, hard-a-starboard, fore half, aft below, five," came the command, and then the first wave of depth charges exploded right above the boat and very close. The water-level glasses shattered, the fuses fell out. And then the next Brit approached, his screws could be heard plainly. Now he was exactly overhead, the depth charges fell . . .

. . . and the other man awoke with a frenzied cry. He was sweating. It took a while for him to realize where he was and to realize that he had only been dreaming and that everything was already over.

The sun was already high in the sky. He had slept until the day was far advanced.

His heart was beating violently and the harsh explosion of the depth charges still rang in his ears. In front of his eyes, he still had the picture of the people swimming around and the outlines of the destroyers as they came surging up to the boat.

And now?

He was panting. He could not simply dive now. Now, he was sitting on the dinghy and the sun was burning like the devil, but otherwise there was nothing else there. Nothing, absolutely nothing. Only water and sky, the empty horizon and the rubber dinghy, and him with his inflamed throat. "Nothing in sight, my friend," he said.

Or? Over there on the port side, wasn't there something floating?

The other man strained his eyes till they hurt even more. There was something indeterminate to be seen on the water in the shimmering sunlight.

Until he finally recognized that it was the one-armed man who was floating over there.

So it was the one armed man.

The other man rested his head on his knees, crouched down, and tried to escape from what was coming towards him, what was coming from within himself and what was coming from outside. He screwed up his eyes so as not to see anything. He put his arms around his head and turned away. The one-armed man was there and he was there to stay. He was floating over there! Why was he floating there? Couldn't he finally disappear? The dead always attack, he recalled, and a cold, cynical anger against the dead man rose up in him.

His thoughts were confused by the one wish he now had, they concentrated themselves on something else and ran abeam. He only had one wish: that the one-armed man would disappear, quickly and at once. But what could he, the other man, do? How could he get rid of him?

He remembered the bottle.

Here, now drink up first, my God, his throat swallowed and the liquor burned, will the whiskey never stop?

He held the empty bottle under the water to fill it up again. What a glug-glug sound it made, and the warm water on his hands, now they were freezing cold again, damn, and where was the one-armed man?

"Now, take good aim, slowly, my friend," he said and weighed the bottle in his hand. It was full and heavy and felt round. He drew his arm back.

Now!

So now: throw.

He threw. But of course the distance was too great. The bottle fell in the water with a dull thud far too short of the one-armed man: it sank immediately.

The other man jumped around in rage. The dinghy rocked and he almost fell overboard.

"Just you wait, you dog!" he shouted. "We'll get you under the water soon enough! I'll show you!" he shouted, blind with rage; he grabbed hold of the paddle and rowed wildly towards the one-armed man.

He was so enraged that he no longer felt thirsty or weak. There was an empty space in his skull that commanded his arms to row towards the floating body. He could not feel his arms and suddenly sweat was running over his dried-out body again. His lungs were red-hot and he felt nothing. He felt absolutely nothing. He kept raising himself up and making for the one-armed man floating on the water, shouting out a few words and then rowing on, groaning with the effort.

The alcohol flooded his brain more and more. He had drunk up all that was left in the bottle and now the liquor was melting away in his stomach, penetrating his whole body, expanding and flooding everything and ratcheting up his strength.

His arms worked like a windmill with the paddle. The dinghy was wet with spray from his paddle-strokes in the water, but he maintained his course perfectly, without any deviation, towards the one-armed man.

[65]

Until he got close to the dead man floating on the water.

He stopped rowing, rose up, and needed a moment to regain his balance. He raised the paddle high in the air and wanted to puncture the one-armed man so that the gas would escape and he would disappear into the depths.

Just as he was about to strike the blow, he stopped. Something grabbed hold of his arm. He dropped the paddle.

Because he had looked at the one-armed man and could now not go ahead with it. The one-armed man was the one-armed man again and no longer the dead man. He had changed back again.

The paddle now lay in the dinghy and the other man stood with his head down and looked at the one-armed man.

The one-armed man was floating along quietly. The other man and the rubber dinghy were of no concern to him. He was not interested in what was trying to approach him. His healthy arm hung down in the water, pointing down into the depths. Of course the body was heavier on that side. And on the lighter side, the stump of his arm stuck out of the water and pointed to the sky. The one-armed man's face also lay on its side, one half under water, the other dry in the air. The face. It had been the face that had said "Stop!" The face and not the stump, as terrifying and repellent as that looked. No, that was not what it was. But the face. What was there in the one-armed man's face? Now he simply couldn't do it.

The dead man's face was peaceful and had a different expression from what it had had before, when he was still alive, and later on, when he was already dead but still on board the dinghy. The face was completely different, it had departed and was more than just "dead." The eyes were open and looked horizontally across the surface of the water. At any rate, the one eye that the other man could see did. And the other eye beneath the water?

The one-armed man's face looked as though he were saying "Now, now, my friend, just be sensible, who would ever let himself go like that! You mustn't do that, what's going to happen to you otherwise? Come on, old man, be careful and keep your senses!"

The other man looked suspiciously at the dead man's face to see if, perhaps, it was smiling or was perhaps making fun of him. But the face stayed still and supercilious, the other man could not make anything out. He could only see the one-armed man floating along in his solitude. He tried, as he had done before, to be angry and to laugh derisively, but he was unsuccessful and he was glad that he was unsuccessful. And yet, in spite of it all, the alcohol danced in the recesses of his brain. Everything appeared unreal and was like a crazy dream.

He sat down on the side of the dinghy and let his legs dangle overboard in the water and looked at the one-armed man.

So, there he was floating in the water.

"Dear one-armed man," he said. "So now I am sitting here and looking at you. I am still alive. For how long? How long will it be before I am floating in the water like you?"

There was the one-armed man floating, his legs pointing diagonally downwards, slightly apart.

And then the other man felt sick to his stomach. He had discovered little herring-like fish under the dead man's body and saw that they were bumping up against the floating body with their little round mouths and noses and had already eaten part of the healthy arm.

The alcohol in the other man's stomach began to churn again. He doubled up a little. Then he quickly swung his legs back into the dinghy, took a deep breath to give his stomach some room, and then rowed as fast as he could away from the partially eaten corpse. He sat with his back towards the floating body and had the feeling that it was following him. He rowed and paddled again, fearful and disgusted and panting and groaning with all the alcohol in his blood and with no clear thoughts except to get away from there.

The sun was standing a little before its zenith when he had to stop. He couldn't do any more. He was done in, completely done in and exhausted. He had stopped and was squatting in one corner of the rubber dinghy, hiccupping with exhaustion and not daring to look around, to see whether the dead man was still close behind him, whether he was there at all, how far away from him he was, whether the one-armed man had perhaps followed him . . . perhaps he had come on board and was even sitting behind him!

With a jerk he turned around, ready to scream and to strike. But there was no one there. There was nothing there. In him and around him, nothing.

His breath whistled with the exertion and his body was deaf, as though set aside by weakness.

"Oh, my God!" was all he could think, over and over again.

Until this too stopped and the liquor gained the complete upper hand inside him and set the rest of his reason aside.

He began to imagine things, sometimes laughing out loud, sometimes high and sometimes low, and violet and red rings of color appeared before his eyes.

His thoughts swelled up and began to be amused at what had just happened. He grew indifferent to everything. He sang, most beautifully and off-key, a long, drawn-out passage, the high notes ornamented with double trills. He sang "O du mein lieb Heimatland" ("O thou, my dear homeland") and "Wem Gott will rechte Gunst erweisen" ("To whom God really wishes to show favor"), and he expanded the text like a folk song. It didn't matter what he sang and whether it was right. What he sang was right.

"It's right, do you hear!" he shouted.

And it was Christmas, "Kinderlein kommt" ("Come little children") and "Oh, Christmas Tree!" he sang, "how brown are your leaves." "That comes from the Party" he said. "The brown leaves."

He choked with laughter.

"Brown Christmas in the Atlantic," he sang, and ornamented the melody.

He suddenly stopped singing. He rose a little unsteadily and put his finger to his nose. He was seeking clarity, and as he spoke it was though a knife were cutting through his throat.

"You're drunk, my dear friend!" he said to himself and bowed. "Dear me!"

He was too warm. He tore his shirt off his body and took off his pants. Damn, damn, damn the sun. He stood in the middle of the rubber dinghy, naked, and screamed at the sun. He had forgotten the one-armed man. Now it was the sun that was enraging him and the heat that embittered him.

"You want to do me in, don't you?" he screamed at the sun. "Just don't go getting any ideas, you with your fire! Where did you get your fire, eh? What else can you do? Well, where did you get your fire? All right, I'm waiting. No answer?"

He waited. The sun said nothing.

"Then I'll tell you!" he screamed, and his voice cracked. The knife was cutting and burning in his throat. He lowered his voice. On account of the pain and because he was making too much noise for himself to say what he wanted to say.

"Autogeny is what it's called," he said mysteriously, put his finger to his nose again, and looked fixedly at the sun. "Autogeny, my friend, the creation of energy from oneself, that's what it's called. Or are you perhaps a hermaphrodite? Or did some deus ex machina impregnate you? No? You see!"

His voice was raised again and grew distorted: "So, that's what you are. And you want to burn me up? You as the creatrix of all life? Dea solis, eh?"

[69]

The other man shook with laughter. Ha-ha. You shouldn't laugh at it, should you?

He couldn't calm down. The paroxysm of laughter ended up as a convulsion. He turned around and bent over. His body was a sea of fire. It was burning and crackling, it gnawed at him and stung him and rattled up from bottom to top.

He lay on the bottom of the dinghy and hugged his knees with his arms. But it was no use. His stomach was like a stone, hard and merciless. His legs twitched and his arms could no longer hold anything. His head wagged and shook. And then he threw up. He could feel it welling up within him and he wept with rage. But there was nothing he could do. He tried to shout, shout something terrible. But the cry was suffocated by what came out of his stomach. His head tipped to one side. He felt himself drifting off, somewhere, drifting, my God, how lovely. There was no body, no stone, and no fire any more.

"I'm falling," he tried to say. "How lovely!" Then, sobbing, he let himself fall.

Bile, green and poisonous, spilled over his lips, out of his mouth. But he did not see or feel it anymore. He was just drifting and it was beautiful, wonderfully beautiful. A sweet and tender sound of music welled up. Something surrounded him. "My darling, what is it?" He tried to think. Perhaps it was Maria? But he could not recognize anything anymore. Only the music sounded, deep, sonorous, and magnificent, and carried him away, and a broad space opened up, warm and soft. From the distance came a long echo.

The other man lost consciousness. He lay on the bottom of the rubber dinghy. He was naked. Vomit ran in little ribbons over his body and was quickly dried out by the sun. There were only little crumbly crusts left on his skin.

The other man's face was beautiful and relaxed.

The one-armed man floated in the water at a fixed distance from the dinghy. He did not approach the dinghy and he did not go further away. The only thing that happened was that his direction changed from time to time: a little more forward, then back again, with the current.

And so they went on next to one another, the dead man and the other man. The horizon was clear and unobscured. There was nothing in sight.

4

He came around from his faint only just enough to be conscious of the fact that he was intoxicated.

He felt well. There was a pleasant warmth in his body and he did not feel the heat outside of him. His thirst was concealed beneath the alcohol as though under a cloak. His thoughts drifted wonderfully; if he kept his eyes shut there was a gentle rocking in his head. It was so beautiful that he did not want to move. There was a buzzing and a sound of music in his ears. "Someone's thinking about me." That was what they had always said as children.

Someone's going to come along any minute and say "Get up," he thought. And I'm so gloriously tired.

He breathed deeply.

"Where did you drink so much?" he tried to recall. Where on earth had he been?

He concentrated his thoughts, but nothing occurred to him. At Chez Elle, perhaps? Or in the Atlantic Bar? And who else was there?

He felt carefully all around himself; perhaps someone was sleeping next to him? Perhaps it was a girl whom he had picked up somewhere last night? Or someone else? No. There was no one there.

"That's good," he said. "That's a good thing, old man," he said. "That's not going to happen again, eh?"

He tried to concentrate. But his thoughts were all at sixes and sevens and were not coherent.

I must get back on board, he thought. Good Lord, when are we actually going to set sail? If I only knew where we were yesterday evening. I remember seeing Charlie, yes, he was sitting in the gutter without his jacket and shoes with some woman on his arm. Charlie, if the patrol catches you, be careful and don't drink so much. It's not good for you, Charlie! Now you're sitting in the gutter telling the woman your old stories, when you were still a navigation officer on the *Columbus*. Don't drink so much, d'you hear? If I only knew where we were yesterday evening.

He pricked up his ears for a moment. What was that droning? There was something droning, wasn't there?

It must be the ventilators. The chief engineer is airing out the boat. That's the right thing to do. How late is it, actually? Are they cleaning ship up there on the deck?

He was too lazy to open his eyes and look at his wristwatch.

It must still be early enough, he thought, and smiled. Where can Maria be? She likes to come creeping into my cabin to see me in the mornings. How many more days furlough do I have left, actually? Don't think about it. Don't be so childish, Maria! You can't let little girls get freezing cold in the cool of the morning, so come along. How long has my bedroom had a ventilator? Are you still cold, Maria? But surely there is something droning?

Every one of the four engines of a four-engine bomber has about two thousand horsepower. The bomb load carried by the plane depends on the length of time taken by the mission it has been ordered to carry out. Reconnaissance flights are not very popular in the USAF, they're considered to be a boring business with little excitement.

The plane had started out in the morning. The crew members were dozing, with the exception of the pilot, of course. The coast was soon out of sight. And now beneath them there was only water all around. Their first task was to fly reconnaissance over the mid-Atlantic—what a silly business. Recently the squadron had lost a plane, heaven knows where it was. The whole group had searched for it for two days and had found nothing.

Now they were flying their reconnaissance, free to hunt U-boats. This evening they would be back home again. Always the same old thing. And that's what they call war! To hell with bloody Hitler.

The radar was switched on and showed nothing. What was there for it to show? U-boats were down here only on very rare occasions and then individually, and they could hardly be caught, especially not when the visibility was super-clear.

They had eaten. The bombardier was brewing up some strong coffee. "Coffee's ready," he announced, and came creeping forward. The pilot switched to automatic pilot, the radio operator came out of his little cabin, and the others all gathered around the coffee too. The sergeant navigator passed cigarettes around and it was nice and comfortable.

Then it was time to change course by 180 degrees. Everybody went back to his station. They scanned the horizon and the surface of the water, but there was nothing in sight. After three hours, another change of course, this time in the direction of home. "Well, we've made it," said the radio operator and radioed their position to the control tower. Everything OK. They were on their way home again and the crew began daydreaming about the evening.

Mabel will be waiting, thought the first pilot, she really is overanxious. Wonder what there'll be for dinner? Mabel always has some nice surprises up her sleeve. Freddy, the bombardier, was worried about his progeny. The baby might arrive at any moment and Mary had such a narrow pelvis; let's hope everything's all right.

The radio operator actually had no one at home. But he knew exactly where he would go. The chief girl at the Blue Chinese liked him. "No other man," she had said yesterday, and oh, boy! She kept her word.

Aft, Freddy was thinking that the rear gunner was a nut case, but he liked him very much in spite of that. He reads Old English poems and French stuff and books by the damn Krauts, no civilized person could remember the titles. Oh well, leave him be.

Towards evening, the bomber prepared for landing at its home base. Everything had gone off well. Mission accomplished and nothing seen.

Every crew member went home, or in the direction where he thought he belonged. The radio operator drank a wonderful champagne with the chief girl. Freddy, in the meantime, had acquired a boy, and Mary was in very good health, thank God. The copilot got drunk in solitude and sat meditating until he fell over. The first pilot soon fell asleep. Mabel was still awake lying beside him and was looking at his face. The rear gunner couldn't get to sleep and sat reading in bed.

"The passing bell rang at one o'clock," he read.

"I woke up startled from my dream," he read.

"The night sky was covered in stars as never before," he read.

"I saw my head covered with mildew like a mushroom and my chest was stuck full of knives," he read.

"I slept until a clap of thunder wakened me."

He looked the quotation up in the index. "Klabund," said the rear gunner. "Never heard of him." And then he switched the light off and still couldn't fall asleep.

———

The other man had heard the droning. Somewhere, far off, there was a sound of droning, it grew louder, very loud, and then quickly died down again.

"Those disgusting ventilators!" he said to Maria. He would complain about them later on. There was no peace, not even here.

"You can't even sleep as long as you like when you're on leave," he said to Maria.

And then he noticed that Maria was not next to him.

The alcohol inside him grew weaker and the earlier images faded away. Even Charlie with his woman had disappeared. There was absolutely no one there.

The other man opened his eyes. It took all his might to force himself to do this. He looked around and saw too that there was no one there now.

Now he knew once more where he was and in what state. He felt where and how he was lying, the straining of the bottom of the dinghy beneath him and, on his hands, the rough, porous feel of the dinghy's rubber.

The heat encircled his body like a snake, long and repellent. Spiral upon spiral. The sun's fire penetrated to his innermost bones.

He saw that he was naked. He felt ashamed. When he saw the remains of what had come out of his stomach, he was repelled again. The dried bits of vomit, which had turned brown, made his mouth water, but the spittle was not wet; it just gave a sense of strangulation.

He raised his head and looked at the horizon again. Hadn't something droned? Or had he merely dreamed that something had? Of course he'd just dreamed it.

"Of course," he said aloud, and covered up his nakedness. Every movement hurt and took a great effort. His skin seemed to burn and he no longer knew when and why he had undressed. Such madness, to lie down naked in the sun!

[76]

"Adam in Paradise," he said, and once more the old scripture grew stronger within him.

"Adam in Paradise. He has eaten the apple and now he is ashamed," he said, and pulled his pants on again.

He laughed when the thought occurred to him: Was Adam ashamed because of Eve or because of the serpent?

"We'd better leave that problem to old Weininger. Hadn't we?" he said. "The main thing is that you've got some pants to put on."

He got up. The dinghy rocked. He was not steady on his legs and he had a headache. He sucked his breath through his teeth. His body ached with thirst. He knelt down and poured water over his head and shoulders. At first the seawater was as sharp as a knife and took the skin off his body. But after that it was wonderfully cool and the pain subsided. He breathed more easily and had to make a huge effort not to drink the seawater. If he were to drink the water, he would be finished within a few hours, he knew that for a fact.

Seawater is a solution of different salts that give it its bitter, salty taste. Its smell comes mainly from decaying organic substances. The main components of sea salt are sodium chloride (cooking salt), about 77 percent; magnesium chloride, about 10 percent; magnesium sulfate, about 5 percent. A kilogram of seawater contains about 35 grams of salt and is thus not suitable for drinking. The consumption of large quantities of seawater can lead to severe disorders, which, in the case of persons dying of thirst, can lead to madness. There is a certain comic side to this, in that a person on the sea is surrounded by water and can still die of thirst.

He looked only at the sun. Noon was long past and he had as yet drunk nothing. His body contracted when he thought of the whiskey. Where was the bottle?

It was not where it had always been. He looked. Where else could the bottle be? He didn't need to look for long, there was almost nowhere here where one could look for anything. He did not find the bottle. It was not there.

He sat on the padding on the side looking straight ahead, stupidly. Where had the bottle gotten to?

When it became apparent to him that he now had nothing more to drink, he felt a movement beneath his skin and he saw the way the hairs on his arm stood up as if the skin were freezing cold. Little goose bumps formed at the roots of the hairs. He shook himself. He could not focus his thoughts and think exactly where the bottle could have gone. Then his skin began to hurt again. The seawater on it had been dried up by the sun. And now the skin on his shoulders had begun to grow taut. Little frail white outlines of saltwater had been left on the hairs on his chest.

"The water evaporates," he said, "and I remain. The salt of humanity."

He sat down so that the sun could not reach his back. It was a bit more bearable that way.

"Salt of humanity," he repeated. A merry thought. And him of all people?

Then it finally occurred to him what had happened to the bottle. That was the end, he knew, and he felt faint.

"Finis omnium," he said. "Curtain up on the last act." Just like Schiller, he thought. At the end there are only dead people left. The only difference is that we cannot take a bow after the final curtain. What was it the ancient Romans used to say? "Plaudite amici." You were very attentive in school.

He lit himself a cigarette. Four cigarettes and a piece of chewing gum were now all that he had left.

He held the cigarette between two fingers and saw that his hand was shaking.

"It's not nearly so simple when the end is coming so fast, is it?" he said to his hand.

He tried to hold his hand still. But he couldn't. He held the hand that held the cigarette with his other hand, but it only shook more.

The cigarette was dry and crackled when he drew on it. The tobacco smoke was a soft silver blue and grey and hung gracefully in the sunlight.

"It tastes as if I've been eating putty," he said, and drew the smoke deep into his lungs. As he took the deep breaths he felt as though the skin on his chest and his back were being ripped off. Yet it felt good.

He smoked and thought about things. Something had to happen now. He couldn't just go on sitting there doing nothing and waiting. The bottle was gone. All right, there's nothing to be done about that.

"You must always take account of the actual state of affairs," he said and grinned at the quotation from his uncle's maxims about life. He had been a practical man and had made his mark in the world. You could always rely on what he said.

"All right, then take account!"

What was left for him to do? Damn little.

He considered: it was now late afternoon. The night should not pose any problems, I can manage that. But during the day tomorrow? I must stay awake tonight, then I can sleep through the day tomorrow, that's the best solution. I'll be able to last through the next night as well. But then?

"Time passes cheerfully," he said and he was no longer grinning. "Evening, night, morning, day, evening, and so on. Everything passes. And no one comes. Time passes and there is nothing in it to pass with it. Except for me. Earlier on, there were all sorts of things that could be lost within time. Here, there is nothing more to lose. Only yourself."

He listened to his breathing and counted the breaths. Each breath was unrepeatable and was gone. Each breath brought him closer.

Closer? You already know where to, he thought, and stopped counting. His lungs went on busily breathing, as though nothing had happened.

He smoked. He had to do something immediately. He could no longer go on thinking about when it would all be over.

He looked along the horizon. He stood up so that he could see better. But there was nothing in sight. He remembered the dead man again. The one-armed man must still be floating around somewhere out there. No, he was no longer to be seen.

"So, all alone," he said.

"Alone," he said louder and very slowly and listened to the sound afterwards.

He threw the cigarette butt overboard. Didn't he want to do something?

He took the one-armed man's wallet out again. He put Betsy's letter to one side. He would read that later. Take it slowly. He had time. He tried the fountain pen. The pen worked excellently. No wonder, a Parker 21, see! He scribbled on the memo pad and then laughed when he saw what he had written. Of course he had written his name. "The name is indeed the most important thing," he said. "If there is nothing else, there is always a name, even if the man is called Müller VIII."

His thoughts had finally turned to what he was going to do now. But he was looking at himself now as though he were standing beside himself. As though he were looking at a stranger.

After he found a ten-dollar bill in the wallet, he cried, "That's just what I needed! Money! Waiter, a beer!"

My God, how silly it was, suddenly to have money here.

Money, well, this was just the right place and the right time for money.

He examined the bill carefully and smelled it.

"The typical stench," he said. "The stench that people like so much. Waiter, where's my beer?" he shouted. "D'you have change for ten dollars?"

"Careful, careful," he said to himself, for the idea of beer troubled him. The vision of several glasses of beer, golden and dewy on the outside from the cold and with little white heads. He swallowed again. Keep on thinking about money, he reasoned, that's the way for it to pass the soonest. He smelled the money again, and the smell actually took his mind off the image of the beer. A repellent smell. A lovely smell.

"Dear money," he said, leaning back and crumpling up the bill. And then he thought of something wonderful.

"The cigarette is worth that!" he cried, and lit the bill with a match. Then he lit his cigarette with the burning ten-dollar bill. He balanced the bill on each corner so that it would burn completely. While the bill was burning, he imagined the people's faces. What they would be saying! Naturally the people would say, "You must have gone mad!" And the businessman, otherwise so friendly, tried to take the money away from him. If the number was still undamaged, the bank would do an exchange. Exchange? The bill or the businessman? The other man was thoroughly enjoying himself; he was having fun.

Or the little girls who were after money like the devil? No, people would just have him locked up. Anyone who burns money is crazy. That's obvious. The man who burns money is a fool. And then. Look at the people's eyes! Money's being lost, their eyes say, better give it to me, me, me . . .

Those are very pathological traits in your thinking, the other man was pleased to note . . . but the people's eyes. Like suckers, looking at the money; where was it that he had seen those eyes in all their clarity? Surely he knew them?

Of course, it had been in Zoppot,* when the war had only been on for a short while. In the casino.

He was playing baccarat and had no idea how the game was played. From time to time he asked the croupier to play for him. The stakes were generally very high. He was sitting next to an immaculately dressed man who was apparently a brick manufacturer, at least that's what he looked like. He ordered a beer and was observing the elegance of the croupier's hands as he handled the cards with lightning speed. He gathered every-thing in—money, chips, cards—with a large, broad knife; the way he did it was really artistic. When the knife passed over the table, people ducked and watched their money disappear. A small, wizened man whose eyes had the look of atropine held the bank. He sweated as he took his three cards out of the box. Everyone looked at the hidden cards as though hypno-tized, and the croupier was holding his knife as if at any mo-ment he might chop someone's head off. The brick man was smoking with moistened lips. The ladies were wearing full-length evening gowns and smelled of perfume. Their jewelry was doubtless genuine. "Ça va!" said the croupier and swept the table clean with his knife. The wizened man had been lucky. People breathed again and looked at the money they had won. The game went on. He had gone over into the India bar, squatted in the corner at the narrow bar counter, and ordered something strange-sounding from the coal-black barmaid. He drank the barbarically sharp drink and still couldn't take his eyes off the gaming table. He drank a lot and quickly. Finally everything seemed to consist only of eyes. The walls of the bar twinkled at him familiarly from a thousand eyes. The men and women in the bar looked at one another like the images on five mark coins. Meanwhile the barmaid had fed him a lot of lies

*A seaside resort on the Baltic, with a casino.

[82]

about her life and was drinking diligently with him. The piano player was hacking out his five-finger exercises in tango tempo.

He got drunk so as finally to forget the eyes. When he left, it was already beginning to grow light. The morning air was wonderful. He walked as far as the head of the long landing stage. He waited until the sun had risen. Then he went back on board.

He had never forgotten the eyes.

So he knew the eyes. And the whole thing had become infinitely banal. Even in his memory, that night was stupid and senseless. How could he have spent his time so stupidly?

The ten-dollar bill was completely burnt and he threw the ashes overboard. So now he no longer had any money. He felt relieved.

He stopped fiddling with the wallet for a moment. It was already beginning to get dark again, thank God. His arms and shoulders were a little less painful. Only where his pants rubbed was there a strong burning sensation. He moved as little as possible.

Giant cumulus clouds lay on the western horizon. In the east it was already blue-grey again. He sniffed the wind.

Wind?

Wind, yes, my God, a small breeze had come up.

He stared at the water. It was being ruffled by minute squalls, scarcely recognizable, and had lost its flat mirror-like surface, the deadly motionless lead-like mirror surface. He turned his face to the wind. He felt it clearly: wind. He was not deceived. The wind breathed gently upon his face. He had the feeling that he was wearing an infinitely thin silk mask. He tasted it with his tongue. Was there moisture in the air? But he could not determine whether there was or not. He was excited.

If bad weather were to come, wonderful, perhaps it would rain, not this damn sun anymore!

Just at that moment, the sun disappeared behind the clouds on the horizon. Distinct clusters of rays pointed upwards into the sky as it was coloring. The rims of the clouds glowed golden, and in the east, black clouds were gathering.

He was excited. His heart was beating fast and he was breathing deeply.

If it rains, he thought, the whole dinghy will fill with water! Then I can go on for a long time. That would be a joke, wouldn't it?

He lit his penultimate cigarette. He had to do something to celebrate the wind.

His thirst grew stronger as he thought about rain and water. His stomach felt as though it were boiling. He swallowed repeatedly.

The sun had now completely disappeared behind the clouds. The sky was reeling in burning colors. Olive green, and light blue, and violet, and black and white, and pink, and, superimposed on all the colors, ox-blood red. The sky was wearing itself out with its color games. The mixture of color tones changed minute by minute. And now they were as ceremonial as a church window, a deep rich red and a radiant dark blue. The great window behind the altar in the cathedral. Wasn't that music playing? The organ is playing, listen, and the choir is singing! Those pious boys' voices, and it is Christmas and the message from on high, "Es ist ein Reis entsprungen" ("A shoot has sprung"), is what they are singing, and it echoes in the high vaulted roof.

The other man closed his eyes in rapture. He stopped swallowing. The peacefulness of the church and the heavenly song were behind his eyes. There is nothing more beautiful than boys' voices, he thought. And they sang the age-old message of the "Reis entsprungen."

He had always gone to the Christmas service with Maria. Just because of the choirs. He was less interested in what the preacher said from the pulpit. Just the choir. Just the music. Do you hear, Maria? It's nice to cry, isn't it? And why are there tears in our own eyes, what nonsense, a man and tears. That's not something that happens nowadays. Can you hear what the minister is saying at this moment? All right, let him be. The people need it. He's talking about our heroes who have fallen in the war, every one of whom was carrying the New Testament in his pack. That's a sheer lie, isn't it? Soldiers carry socks and undershorts in their packs, perhaps a spare pair of shoes as well. Out there in the field, that's more important. Perhaps they do sometimes have a little book in the side pocket. Depends on their temperament. I'm sorry, Maria, that's a bad word: temperament. I knew some people who carried a copy of Baudelaire with them, or *Hyperion,* or Niels Lyhne, a few of Gottfried Benn's poems, or, most often, an issue of *True-Life Experiences,* or also, very often, the familiar postcards of Madame Lamour. Yes, that's what they carried with them. Not what he's talking about up there in front, or at least not in the way he says it. Look at how the light of the church window strikes the crucifix. Can you see? He can't do anything about what they are doing to him. Now it's over. We're going home, right? Quite slowly through the snow-covered park.

The other man cast his eyes upwards again. The sky was still only dark blue. The stars had come out and the wind had become more noticeable. Very small waves that the wind had stirred up pushed the dinghy towards the southwest. The other man was finally on course.

He lay down in a corner of the dinghy, bent over on his stomach because the thirst made it hurt so much. He waited.

"Dear God," he said, "let it rain soon."

And then he was ashamed. Because of that earlier Christmas. But what did that have to do with God, he thought. Afterwards, when he had thought it all through, he was no longer ashamed.

He lay like this for a long time in the gathering night. Thirst was already making his thoughts somewhat confused without his noticing it.

Night had fallen, and he could no longer determine whether the wind had grown stronger or whether it had subsided. The dinghy seemed to be rolling lightly. A pleasant movement! Every nerve of his body felt the movement. He raised himself up so that he could feel it more distinctly. He found it very hard to get up and he noticed how weak and empty he had become.

So now he was standing there looking across the water and feeling the wind and the sea all around him and feeling the way it was moving. He was floating in a particular direction and he would arrive somewhere and he would be found, and at last it would be all over.

And Maria will no longer be there, not at the place I arrive at, he thought. He was overwhelmed by a great sorrow when he thought of Maria.

"Love," he said.

She would not be there, in spite of the wind and the rain, even if he really did arrive somewhere. She would not be there.

The other man was no longer standing so upright.

Up to now, he hadn't thought of that.

I'm standing here and yet where am I actually? he thought. One way led to Maria? And one way led away from Maria? Or was it different?

"To be or not to be, that is the question!" he said, cynically and full of anger.

"It's easy to set someone down at the crossroads," he said, and it was so hard for him to speak, it was as though he had glue in his throat. "And then to give the verdict in retrospect, to judge and condemn, from the judge's golden throne, eh? You make it very easy for yourself, my dears."

To whom was he speaking, actually?

He pondered. Hadn't he once said something similar? Here on the dinghy?

He tried to remember. Of course, now he recalled.

He bent slowly over and sat down again. It was good to be able to sit down.

As he moved, he felt that everything was leaving him. The last remnants of his strength ebbed from him, like water from a vessel. What remained within him grew smaller and smaller. The hollow within him spread, and what was running out of him grew bigger and bigger. The feeling of being empty caressed him like a soft hand, from his head down over his body, finishing at his extremities.

He settled down a little more so that he was resting, half recumbent, near the padding on the side.

He knew that he would never stand up again. Yet he tried to discern the horizon and scan it. But there was nothing in sight.

The wind had dropped again, and the sea was as it had been before. Only the clouds on the horizon were a little thicker than usual.

What is understood by the concept "hope" is a wish for something in particular, irrespective of whether that wish can or cannot be fulfilled.

Hope is one of life's strongest motivating forces and can, in borderline cases, even be identified with the urge for self-preservation.

The usual religions have always intimately interwoven their concepts of the divine and their credos with those aspects of hope that support their promises.

5

The other man was still lying down peacefully and a deathly hush surrounded him. The sound of the waves had ceased and the sea spread out motionless. It had probably only been a squall coming from the upper levels of the air. The night sky was just like the night sky of the previous nights, a dark blue satin with the infinite luster of the stars.

The other man lay quietly and looked up at the sky. His body was deaf and hollow and yet his lying there felt harsh and clear. He could no longer speak. He had tried once or twice, but when all he heard was a croak he had given up. Besides, speaking out loud wasn't important. On the contrary, he found that the silence all around him, and within him, did him good. Of course he still spoke, but he heard his speech only within himself, in his own ear. But he had to speak, for when he spoke to himself in this way it was more than just thinking; a mellowing filter had been inserted. Speaking out loud could be bad—and actually, in his case, always had been, as he now realized—and thinking was mostly imprecise and encumbered by its own special "feeling," as he also discovered when he was talking silently to himself.

"A strange situation," he said. He had never experienced this before. External things scarcely made any impression on him any more. He only felt the pain in his swollen throat as though that glued-up throat were not his own. The thirst in his body was like a strange book that he had left lying unopened. The only clear thing that he felt was the cold in his hands, for they had fallen into the water, from the rubber padding down into the water. He needed all his remaining strength to lift his hands up till they once more lay on the padding. And then, for safety's sake, he pulled them back close to him inside the dinghy. Now they were lying next to him on the wooden bottom of the dinghy and were still a bit cold as they were drying. And he thought of Maria again.

Until Maria was suddenly there and looking at him.

She leaned forward and blew gently on his hands. The drying out no longer hurt. He sighed. Maria's breath on his hands, my God . . .

When he was finally able to open his eyes, Maria was no longer with him and only the star Betelgeuse was shivering where she had been. A star. Only a star.

And then he began to wait. He lay and waited. Something more than just the passing of time had to happen. Surely he was not lying there like this for nothing?

The longer he waited, the less he had to wait for. The dinghy and the night that was passing began to leave him behind, as though something solid were dissolving in a liquid. He felt as though he were far off, as though he were flying, exploding softly into the faraway surroundings. There was an upsurge within him and an opening beneath him down in the depths. A space inside him opened up, a sort of tangible vacuum within him, and because it seemed so real, he even thought he could seize hold of it with his hands. And in the midst of this unfilled yet real enough object, he felt himself at one particular point rolled up tight into a ball, shrunken beyond all measure and possessed of an uncanny strength.

He was looking with wide-open eyes far off into the sky above him. The stars twinkled, reflected in his eyes, and yet were far away.

"Now we'll operate on his cataract!" said someone, wickedly and suddenly. The other man could not make out where the voice came from, or whose voice it was.

Betsy was sitting up in bed. Her leg was making good progress. In a few weeks she would be able to get up again.

"There are wonderful false limbs," said the senior doctor and flirted with her as well as he could. "No one will notice that you . . . well, you can even wear nylons on them, and proper shoes of course. Nowadays no one needs crutches any more. But my dear, you're cheating!"

Betsy was playing solitaire on the bed table.

"It never comes out unless you cheat," she said. "I learned that from Hamsun."

The senior doctor knew no one by the name of Hamsun and thought it was one of her admirers. Well, well, and she's engaged.

"Heard anything of William?" he asked.

"No," she said.

What was he to say next? He waited for her to start weeping. But she did not. If she had wept he would have known exactly how to behave, as a kindly comforter. The young girl and the experienced man. But as she wasn't weeping that was no good, and he was angry.

She can cheat if she likes, he thought. Mr. Halmon, or whatever his name is, isn't coming into my house.

The nurse stuck her head around the door. "You are wanted in the operating room," she piped.

"I have to operate," he said importantly and knew what he was capable of. "So long." He took his farewell in the nicest manner. Betsy dealt a new game of solitaire. But the game didn't come out, and she didn't want to cheat any more. She leaned back, pushed the bed table away, and reread her father's last letter. "My dear child," she read, and began to weep. William would no longer like her with this missing leg. "Your dear Pop" she read at the end of the letter. She felt wretched and deserted by the whole world.

"Damn it all," she said and turned the light out. She took a sleeping pill.

If only this thing hadn't happened to my leg, she thought.

"Why do they have to operate on my cataract?" the other man asked, and felt his eyes.

Betsy was now standing where Maria had just been standing. Just as she looked in the picture. She looked at him.

"No," he said, to set her mind at rest, "I haven't read your letter, don't be afraid, Betsy."

He could easily recognize her face. Now, as he looked at it more closely, it was no longer as sweet as in the picture. On the contrary, her face seemed sad. It was like all faces of that sort, very sad.

"I'm sorry," he said. "I didn't know." She smiled like Maria.

"You all look alike," he said, "That's strange."

Betsy had lit a cigarette and was smoking. The cigarette smoke was like a dark cloud against the night sky. She said nothing.

"The one-armed man didn't know that either," he explained. "He was really very angry with you."

She went on smoking.

"Perhaps he knew more than he said? You must know that he had a wonderful death. If I could die like that, I would be happy!"

Betsy stopped smoking for a moment and looked at him. She smiled just like Maria and shook her head. And then she was gone.

The other man looked up at the sky.

The time passes so quickly, he thought. And he tried to catch up with himself. He raised himself high up in the air.

"I'm hovering," he said, "I'm hovering above myself. Look, there I am down there!"

He looked at himself lying stretched out below, both his hands next to each other, his head thrown back and his legs slightly bent. A black dot on the vast mirror-like surface of the ocean.

He hovered even higher. Far below him another dark dot appeared, another rubber dinghy with a man floating in it. And there was another and another and another. A lot of black dots all infinitely far away from one another and as close as the stars in the sky. And a dead face was circling around every one of the rubber dinghies, and an arm that had been shot off, and legs that had been eaten away. Slowly, like moons, they were encircling the dinghies. And none of the men floating there knew about the others, knew that there was someone else floating like himself. And not one of the dead men knew about the others, that there were other dead men with limbs shot off and faces weathered by the water. Every one, whether dead or still alive, floated along in solitude and knew only about himself. Only sometimes—the other man could see this clearly from up above—one of the men floating there knew that a dead man was floating around him and how he was floating.

The other man could no longer look at the sun and drew back into himself again.

He lay in his rubber dinghy, no longer looking at the night sky, and saw the stump of the one-armed man's arm reaching over the rubber edge of the dinghy and pulling his body after it. The dead man came on board.

Everyone is visiting me today, thought the other man, and he was glad.

"That's nice of you," he said. They must know how lonely I

am, he thought, and they come and visit me. Previously, I was always so lonely but no one came to visit me after Maria died. It's nice.

"Hello, my friend!" he said.

The one-armed man climbed slowly on board, and the other man was not in the least surprised that he had come back to him.

"I have never forgotten you," he said to him, "you don't have to believe that, but it's true. I've been thinking of you all the time as you were floating around me out there. And the other thing, my wanting to do something to you, you mustn't take it to heart. You can imagine how I felt, can't you? It wasn't very easy."

The one-armed man had sat down where Maria and Betsy had been sitting. His face was leached out by water and from being dead and it was almost transparent.

"I'm sure I have a fever," said the other man. "Of course I have a fever. Otherwise I wouldn't be seeing all this. That's obvious, I'm seeing ghosts. I must think precise thoughts and consider everything with the greatest care."

He strained his eyes so as to see clearly, yet he felt as though his eyes were shut. He could not see anything and yet he saw everything with exceptional clarity.

"Strange," said the other man, "everyone who visits me smiles at me, as though they were sorry for me."

He was not pleased by the pity.

"I don't need your pity at all," he said to the one-armed man. "If perhaps you do think I need it, then you are mistaken. Just don't worry."

But the one-armed man only shook his head, gently and as though as an afterthought.

Because of the pity, the other man now no longer wanted to see inside himself. The one-armed man disappeared as he had wished.

"You see!" said the other man.

And then he forced open his two real eyes and looked around. The outline of the dinghy was black against the sky and the stars were shining. They were shining with an inconceivable beauty. There was no one on board and he was alone, as he always was.

"You see!" he said again.

He tucked in his chin and slowly turned his head. There was a light border all around the horizon and there was nothing in sight. The sea, as always, was as flat as a mirror. He stuck his tongue out as far as he possibly could so as to feel the wind that had been blowing before. But there was no wind to feel any longer. The clouds over the horizon had shrunk to a narrow, swollen strip.

"You are about to die softly and blissfully, my friend," he said to himself. He felt his lips stretch over his teeth. He saw himself as if he were in a photograph, trying to grin.

Until he was assailed by fear. He remembered how, as a child, he used sometimes to be afraid. At night in his darkened room, the dim corners and the possibility that something might come out of those corners. Like now. If he were to die now and there were to be someone wanting something of him. Someone who could question him, or could do something to him. The great judge was asking, "How often have you been to church? And if you haven't, why not? Have you profited from your talents, and if yes, by how much? And what else?" The questioning simply did not stop.

"A nice questionnaire," said the other man and calmed down a little. But then he grew angry again.

"If you really are him and still have need of questionnaires, then I can do without you, my friend!" he said aggressively.

He listened. Was there someone there?

No one, he ascertained. He stayed silent as he always did. But the form needed to be filled out.

The other man coughed secretly with laughter. Heavens above, how primitive and banal.

And then he grew frightened again, for did not the future depend on the Great I Am? And what would happen to him?

He had not, you see, been to church every Sunday as he was supposed to have been, and indeed the answers to other questions in the questionnaire were not all too positive.

"Positive!" he said fiercely. "Haven't I heard that word somewhere already?"

He was afraid of what the Great I Am might appoint for him.

The fairy stories of purgatory and hell occurred to him, and perhaps they were true and did actually happen after all? You couldn't be sure, the gods were more incalculable than even the different churches, he thought. And the Great I Am especially! "You can be right ten times over, but if the Great I Am says 'No,' you're lost. Humility, yes, by God," said the other man, as loud as he could. "Be humble, love your enemies! Should I perhaps love the Great I Am?"

He was afraid. The black figures were standing around him and threatening him as they had done in his childhood. As soon as he was dead, they would come at him and do something frightful. The dark thing, the unrecognizable thing, came out of the corners at him and stretched out its hands towards him.

All that was needed was to make a light, he thought quickly. Then the dark corners and figures would disappear.

"Click," he said, "now it's light. So where are you?"

It was light. He looked around him in the nocturnal light. There was no one near him. No shadow and no Great I Am and absolutely nothing. He was alone with himself and his fear. And that could not be denied out of existence.

"I only want to go where Maria is." He closed his eyes again. It was a relief when he was finally able to close his eyes again.

A relief as though he were very, very tired. He was tired, dog tired. He felt sleep gradually permeating his whole body. His legs grew heavy and thought gradually dwindled into unconsciousness, spread itself out, and sank out of sight.

But the other man could not sleep. For the one-armed man was immediately in front of his closed eyes again. He was again smiling that wretched sympathetic smile and was again shaking his head.

"Actually you ought to know more about the Great I Am than I do," the other man said to him. "After all, you are dead already. You could actually do something for me, couldn't you?"

But the one-armed man only shook his head again and took out a cigarette and smoked it, his face turned towards the sky. The other man seemed not to exist for him.

"Do you know anything about the Great I Am?" the other man asked. The one-armed man just went on silently smoking.

"There's not a damn person who knows anything about him," said the other man bitterly. "Or nobody wants to know anything. You could help if you wanted to. But no!"

The one-armed man remained persistently silent.

"Just think about Betsy!" said the other man. "At least you could do something to help her!"

The one-armed man smoked more fiercely. The clouds of smoke hid his face almost completely.

"Clouds in front of the face." The other man recited contemptuously. "Very romantic. The only thing lacking is a suitable poem."

The one-armed man just looked at him and grew smaller. His legs disappeared, his body dissolved, his chest sank into the water, and the stump of his arm sank with a hissing sound. That was the only sound to be heard, the hissing sound of the stump. His head was raised up above the edge of the dinghy. For a short moment he saw it still floating on the water. Then the dead man had disappeared.

"You're crazy," the other man said to himself. "It's gone that far. You're dying and you're seeing stupid things. You're seeing what is simply not there. Such nonsense, dead people coming on board. They're somewhere quite different. I am the only reality here." He couldn't even find the word "reality" funny any longer. That's how far things had gone. He was still frightened of what might possibly happen to him. He felt sure that the shadows were somewhere over there in the corner and were waiting.

The night had grown older and was gradually growing lighter. The stars were losing their deep-yellow glow and were now only transparent dots strewn about in a strange order. The moon's narrow crescent grew pale, and the Southern Cross was sloping and only half over the horizon. Fine veils of mist hovered over the surface of the water and moved gently and infinitely slowly towards the rising sun. A large ray sprang up out of the water near the dinghy, flailed wildly about, and slapped back into the water on its broader side. It sounded like a cannon shot.

The other man lay there, heard nothing, and, with his eyes wide open, looked at the sky as it gradually colored into day.

"Dawn, dawn," he hummed.

Dear old Wilhelm Hauff, he thought. What would Dwarf Nose and little Fatima say about this? Didn't you also have a one-armed friend? He was named Zolenkos, if I'm not mistaken. You see, there are always people somewhere who are lacking something, an arm, often a leg as well, often even their head, often their heart. The cold heart. Don't think about it, my friend, he thought, and now he did begin to weep.

He wept, but there were no tears. When had he last wept? Once as a child when he had had a good hiding? Of course. And otherwise? Once in between. That was a long time ago. There had been a very nasty reason for that, for otherwise grown men do not really weep nowadays, do they, my friend?

[97]

He bared his teeth. It was damn painful. He lay and looked at the morning sky.

The sun had risen and its upper part was above the waterline, and the sky was covered in a kitschy raspberry sauce.

"Bread pudding and raspberry sauce," said the other man, "the typical color of tears."

He was sad.

The day dawned and the other man lay there and could not move. Could he really not move? Wasn't there one more cigarette in the pack? The last one?

Slowly, inch by inch, he stretched his hand out towards the pack of cigarettes. His face was distorted by the effort. He dropped the cigarette a few times before he could get it into his mouth. Striking the match was a new, an intensified, effort. Finally, slowly and painfully, everything fell into place. He knew that he was making every movement for the last time.

"The sun," he said softly and looked at the red, moistly pregnant ball. "The last sun, oh, well . . ."

He had finally succeeded in lighting the cigarette. But the lighted cigarette fell out of his mouth again and lay on his thigh. He looked at it there and waited to see what would happen. The tip burned a hole through the fabric of his pants. He felt no pain in his leg. The burning ash was no longer able to hurt him.

"Well?" he said, and went on waiting.

"All right, then nothing!" he said, and again he had to make an effort to get hold of the cigarette and put it in his mouth. He felt with his fingers to see whether the cigarette was actually, and properly, in his mouth, for he could feel nothing with his lips. He clenched his jaws so as to hold the cigarette in his mouth and only then did he take his hand away. The cigarette stayed in his mouth. So his face was still functioning.

He inhaled the smoke deeply. It oozed through his body

like a slight intoxication. The sun grew green and the sea rose up high.

"Good morning, dear sun! Look, my cataract has been punctured," he said to the sun, and looked straight into its light.

A long time passed.

The cigarette soon went out and was still hanging in the corner of his mouth. He had closed his eyes again and was daydreaming. His body was wonderfully at peace. He was lying as though on a bed made of cotton wool. He did not consciously feel the heat of the sun, which was now quickly gaining strength.

He was daydreaming. His thoughts moved very slowly and quite comfortably from one image to another and then stopped whenever he remembered something especially beautiful, and yet he knew all the time exactly where he was and what state he was in and that he was steadily dying.

Things are strangely juxtaposed, he thought. In spite of it all, he still took a little pleasure and a sly satisfaction when he saw himself lying there as though parallel to himself.

"The time has come to strike a balance," he said. "I cannot close my life while there are still some accounts open. Let's hope it won't be a debit balance!" he said, and the remains of the cigarette moved in the corner of his mouth.

Actually, what do I still have outstanding? he mused.

"Nothing," he said, after exhaustive thought.

That was good. It was not nice having to demand something from other people who were just as poor as he was.

"To whom do I owe anything?" he asked out loud.

His mouth, his throat, and his pharynx were all extremely painful when he really tried to speak. Well, better not, he thought, you can talk like this too. The main thing is that I hear myself and that the person affected understands me. All right, once again, to whom do I owe anything? Now, I should be able to remember. The list is a long one. A lot of people are coming and will want something. All right, they can be given it. But the other people who don't come and want to have something, but who, in spite of that, are still owed something, they are a lot more unpleasant. And, alas, there are many of them.

"Very many," he said. "A bit hard on the conscience."

And of course what I owe them is precisely what I do not have, he thought further. There's nothing to be done with money. But what else could, or should, he use to pay them with? He knew exactly. His hands had not been freezing cold since then for nothing.

"What other liabilities do we have?" he asked, and opened his eyes again. He looked into the fiery noon solar ball.

"None," said the sun. He was nearly blinded by the light and the answer.

"What assets do you still have?" asked the sun.

"None," said the other man, and closed his eyes again. Things were dancing around in his skull and were starting to get all mixed up again.

"But there is some capital!" said Maria.

"But no car," said Betsy.

"The main thing is that you have two arms," said the one-armed man.

"Keep on amusing yourselves!" said the other man. "I'm kibitzing at your game of intellectual skat."

"All you have to do is to like people. Then everything's OK," said Betsy. She had white hair and was a hundred years old.

"It would better if people liked me," said La Gracieuse and her face had fallen.

"I'm dead," said the one-armed man. "That is the only result, whether you're liked or not liked. Look at me! Well?"

"Now, for heaven's sake don't quarrel," said the other man and would have liked to laugh.

Maria waved her hand casually. "Let him die in peace," she said.

"A man may not die without having visited us!" said Betsy wisely, and grew even older.

"They always leave me quickly," said La Gracieuse, and could not understand why.

"Now, just look at the women!" said the one-armed man, and winked at the others.

The other man had finally managed to laugh. And it pierced his chest and he groaned and, of course, there was no one there.

His eyes scanned the horizon as far as they were able. There was nothing in sight. He also tried to scan the horizon behind him, but without success. He could no longer move his head.

He thought a little longer about his balance sheet and then gave up. It was too complicated, he couldn't take it all in. "The Great I Am up there can figure it out better than I can," he said. "After all, he keeps the books."

The cigarette butt in the corner of his mouth twitched again. But the other man quickly grew serious. What was the point of all the nonsense? There were more important things to do now.

He thought for a time. He was still afraid of the darkness, of the Great I Am in the background.

"Actually, why do I keep bothering about the Great I Am?" he asked himself. "Of course because now the need arises!" he said. Such idiocy. I have to start over from a different angle," he said. And then he said, "Nonsense!" I surely can't want to outwit something, he thought. Or look for new ways, now that it's so late.

He had the feeling that the gods, or the Great I Am, were sitting high up above him, looking down on him and taking a magnificent pleasure in his fumblings about and his dying. He grew angry and bitter.

"You can kiss my ass!" he screamed, and then said softly, "I want to end it all decently, nothing more."

And then he snorted and clenched his teeth because a firestorm was racing out of his body. His chest was on fire. A crazy heat was building up in his throat, until it shot out like a cork from a champagne bottle and shattered in his brain. His legs were thrashing about and his hands were hooked on to the bottom of the dinghy, his body was bent upwards in a half-moon. The cigarette butt, however, was stuck firmly in the corner of his mouth and stayed where it was. He had opened his mouth and was breathing jerkily and fast. His thirst was the clapper of a bell and rang like lead in his stomach, the sun was raining burning oil down on him, a flame thrower, and wild images were raging in his brain. The gods embraced one another orgiastically, Maria was laughing shrilly, and a litter of baby dachshunds emerged out of Betsy's lap, what nonsense, and the one-armed man was playing tennis, his racket was floating in the air. Someone was laughing again somewhere, it was not Maria any longer: it was a massive reverberating laugh, re-echoing from all sides, and there they are, the group of laughers, they are all there: old Zeus with Leda on his arm, Odin in Germanic garters, and Jehovah with bloody hands, Allah was shaving, and Buddha was staring at his navel, Manitou with the buffalo heart, and the Negro god was raping Frau Luna. Castles in the moon, a circus, they are all there, always there, and so is the endless laughter, they are having a good time, these swine, and I am dying.

"And I am dying," he said, exhausted.

Hallucinations come, along with other symptoms, when a patient has a fever and is very exhausted (the deliria of inanition). They are perceptions without a corresponding external stimulus, or illusions, i.e., pathologically altered perceptions of real objects. Visual hallucinations are called visions and play a significant role in connection with religion. Hallucinations easily lead to actions that they dictate, such as murder, suicide, and so on. Hallucinations generally consist of numerous images arising from wishes about the future or from an analysis of the past, graduated according to the intensity of the illness or the extent of the brain's exhaustion. Hallucinations are not be confused with meditative states of mind.

"And I am dying," said the other man softly, and then he screamed again.

The group of gods that had assembled did not stop laughing. He looked for the Great I Am but could not find him. He was relieved.

"The Great I Am will teach you what's what!" he screamed at them. "Shove off back where you belong!"

But the group persisted in their laughter. They pointed the other man out to one another, pointed at him with their fingers and then slapped their thighs again with laughter.

"Nirvana," said the other man. "It makes me sick. I hope the Great I Am comes soon."

Suddenly there was silence and the foolishness was wiped away. The other man made an effort to recognize the Great I Am. But he could not see anything. He remembered the cynical thoughts he had had that were to bring the Great I Am to his knees. He did not know what he could say. So he gave up.

"It's not worth it," he said, "what's the point of all this fuss?" He was just glad that the hoard of laughers had disappeared. The silence was good.

He tried to pass his tongue over his lips. But that was no longer possible either. Every movement had grown smaller and was stuck fast in the will to do it. He did not have the strength. His brain was still working well, at any rate, or relatively well.

"Relatively," he said, "well . . ."

That was also a word.

"Only thirst is not relative," he said. "Thirst is absolute, and the rest is nonsense. It's all nonsense."

The sun's rays burned in his brain. But the fear was always present, above and behind everything. He simply could do nothing about the fear.

"That's nonsense, too," he said.

His leg had already been dead when the cigarette burned a hole in it. Now he was dying a little bit higher up.

He spoke soundlessly and chased after the figures that were visiting him.

He grew sad again.

"Nothing's right any more," he said even more sadly. Then he fell asleep again for a while. He hadn't wanted to fall asleep. Perhaps it wasn't sleep, not sleep as generally understood. Everything had simply become different from what it had been previously. What had been right before was no longer right. And vice versa.

"Perhaps that's because of the cataract operation," he said, and he was thankful.

When his body stopped sleeping again, later on, he tried to open his eyes. He knew that he had already raised his eyelids, but he could not see. His eyeballs were turned upwards because of the strain on the muscles and they were looking at what he was still thinking of in his head. The moment he lowered the pupils, his eyelids also lowered and the effort started all over again. He tried to raise his hands and use them to hold on to his eyelids and keep them open. But he could no longer move his hands and they remained indifferent where they were.

The sun was already way beyond noon and was sinking towards the horizon. The sky was spread out blue and without a break. The sea lay brightly polished and did not make a sound. The dinghy turned infinitely slowly on its own axis.

The other man kept trying to see. He strained, hard and embittered, at his muscles. And when he had finally succeeded in opening his eyes, he still saw nothing.

The sun was shining straight down into the middle of his eyes. His eyeballs were dry and his pupils, wide open, looked at the light streaming down. He saw nothing. He knew that he ought to see.

"My eyes are open and I can see nothing," he stated, and was no longer angry. He was only exhausted, nothing more.

"It's not worth it," he said, "there is nothing in sight, in any case."

"Has there ever been anything in sight?" he asked himself. "Earlier, and in general?" he went on to explain, and laughed a little at the expression "in general." "You simply can't avoid expressing yourself so pompously," he said.

"That sounds as though I used to carry on clever conversations at home. That's right though, isn't it?" he asked himself.

"No," he answered.

After he had thought that "no," he went on to muse for a long time. "That used to be true earlier on," he said, "but now?"

He went on thinking about it and again caught himself moving with his thoughts in the direction from which he had come.

"Don't forget!" he warned himself. "You are about to die. And now you're messing around with these things again. You can call them what you like, it's still the same."

He remained silent for a moment.

"Of course there was something in sight," he said. "Wasn't there, Maria? You know there was. I didn't know for a long time. Even now, I sometimes don't know or I forget again. That's because I'm lying here in this condition. And other things too—I'm sorry, Maria—were once in sight. Things about which you know nothing. Tiny little moments. And great big moments. Unfortunately, one only knows these things

[105]

when it's too late. The person who still has time knows nothing, someone once said, I don't know who any longer. And these are the moments that count. Perhaps it's even lucky that you don't always know it at the time it's actually happening."

Now he needed a lot of time for thought. For now, when everything was coming to an end, he could not take things so carelessly. Now, no longer. And he knew that too.

"That's good," he said.

He did not know whether his eyes were open. No, certainly not. His eyelids had fallen down again. It didn't matter, either. He saw different things from the ones that might be out there, outside his own self. He saw a lot of images pass him by in a kindly light. Just as before. Only more beautiful now.

Until his heart began to hurt.

The images gradually disappeared and finally all that was left to him was a blackness, a vacuum before his eyes. He had no time to wonder about it. Instead his thoughts directed themselves like a searchlight toward his heart. What was happening to his heart? Where did this increasing pain come from?

He had to breathe heavily to counteract the increasing pressure. A large hand had emerged from his well-being and had taken his heart between its fingers. And now this hand was closing, slowly and irresistibly, around his heart. The vision of a steel press, as tall as a factory, flashed through his mind.

He could no longer breathe. The pressure was mounting unrelentingly and violently. His heart had no room any longer; it no longer knew how it could emerge from this ever more fearful development and where it could escape to.

It became tighter and tighter. A screw was being tightened, turn by turn. Was there someone there to whom this satanic hand belonged? The Dark One, perhaps? Or the Great I Am? The really Great I Am? Did he take pleasure, perhaps, in closing his hand, in squashing the heart and watching it happen? Like a child tormenting a fly or some other small animal? Tear off a leg, and what does the creature do now? Oops, don't fly away. And just to be on the safe side, let's tear the wings off. What next? Another leg off and then another and another. So, now the little fly doesn't have legs anymore, and it's lost its wings too, the beast is still living though, good Lord! What a buzzing noise it makes. How tough a little beast like that is, you'd never have thought it, would you?

The damn hand squeezed and pressed and closed tighter and tighter. The other man's body began to move. Even the parts that were already dead. The nerves were presumably the cause of these movements.

"Presumably," the other man said in desperation and with difficulty.

"Of course," the one-armed man cried from the bottom of the sea, far away. "Of course the nerves are the cause. Naturally, what else could you have been thinking of?"

"That's the feeling," Maria whispered. He could scarcely understand her, she was so soft and indistinct. He tried to recognize her but could not find her anywhere. He was obviously looking in the wrong direction? Obviously? But her voice was comforting in the midst of the crazy pain.

"Those are the reactions which come from actually being present," said Betsy; she was no longer a hundred years old and had probably forgotten everything again. "The one-armed man has just told you that. He's a doctor, and he knows. You just don't want to believe it, do you?"

The other man's body jerked like a spider's leg that had been torn off. The dark hand was now almost fully closed.

As the final, extreme pressure began and the hand had formed itself into a ball so tight that it could hold nothing more, the other man made a high-pitched, unbalanced whistling sound like a locomotive.

As he screamed, he had forced open his eyes and could see again. He saw that he was sitting upright in the dinghy.

Everything that was still living in and about him was sitting upright in the dinghy and was no longer just lying motionless.

His head jerked as he scanned the horizon. The giant hand was still holding on to his heart. It would not let him go, not to die. He saw everything as if through the wrong end of a pair of opera glasses, stupid and distant and wrong and, my God, wasn't it funny, that's not how you sit or lie there. Posture, what's this all about, that's all wrong, surely?

His eyes scanned the horizon.

The other man could now only distinguish flecks of color. The blue blot up there with the red blob in it, swinging and swaying. The undulating line of the horizon and beneath it the excavated blackness of the sea. High up overhead something white was fluttering.

"Where does that white come from?" he asked himself, and could not think because of the pain. His eyes were fixed on the horizon and he sensed it out along its whole length, like a blind man feeling the curbstone with his cane. But the horizon was empty. There was nothing in front of it on the water. And above it only the sky was glowing.

"Unrestricted view all around!" he said loud and clear. His voice boomed in his ear.

"That was only to be expected," he said, now voiceless, and he could no longer stay sitting upright. He still had a little strength, because the hand around his heart had suddenly gone away and was no longer squeezing. He was not surprised, it was as though he had already forgotten the pain. But he had not forgotten it. He was just looking for the piece of white.

He raised his eyes to where he had previously seen the piece of white. But he could no longer find it in the blue blots.

"They operated on my cataract," he said, "so I really ought to be able to see."

And then he knew, without having seen it again, that it was the Great I Am. The piece of white.

He closed his eyes and went on sitting there. He waited, tried to order his thoughts, and was excited. He had no idea how much time would pass before he would be able to see the piece of white again; then, suddenly and unexpectedly, it was there again, high up in his closed eyes. The piece of white was no longer surrounded by all the blue. It was like being in a movie theater, a white screen. He was sitting in the front row, he had to crane his neck. It was flickering. A strange show, he thought. I should have sat in a better, more comfortable, seat. What has the Great I Am planned? he wondered.

"Just like being in a real movie theater," he said.

The show began. First the commercials. They weren't worth it, silly as always. Then the newsreel. There was an express train; it went so fast that it arrived before it had started. Change of picture. Winter sports, the minister, an ape was doing tricks, the audience was laughing. "The audience always laughs," he said. And what was all this about, anyway?

The show stopped immediately and the other man was pleased. It hadn't been the Great I Am then, this film? Was it the Dark One wanting to frighten him? Still, even now?

The other man could no longer keep sitting upright and fell back into his old position. He felt very relieved when he was able to lie down again as he had before. His heart was no longer painful. Rather the opposite. The hand had gone away. No, on the contrary, it was back again. But differently and not unpleasant, as it had been before. He could hear the quiet beating of his heart. He no longer felt any fear of the dark figures in the corners.

"Corners?" he said. "Where are there any corners here?" He looked around and of course there were no corners.

Of course? he thought. Strange, I was still afraid earlier on and now I've just seen the Great I Am, and who was it who actually put on that movie just now? Who wanted to bluff, and why?

He could not distinguish one from the other. But it wasn't so important. All he felt was that the hand was back again and that the Great I Am was holding his heart so pleasantly. A wonderful peace permeated his whole person, a broad, soft surface. He felt the peace and the beauty of it at every single point in his body. He tried not to speak and not to think. For otherwise he would be destroyed. All he could do was keep quiet. And look at the white light, see how the Great I Am, crossing the sky, was approaching in a flat curved trajectory, and see the way in which the light was increasing without being blinding.

The other man looked at what was coming and closed his eyes. He had grown so tired that he could no longer keep his eyes open. It was enough that he knew it was approaching him. And if he were now to sleep a little? He would be awake again when the light reached him.

But he could not sleep. The silence was too great. The noise of his own body in his ears had finally ceased. And everything around had grown quiet.

He kept silent. Only the images passed by him as in a dream, as they had before, but differently; images, darkened and deepened by the smoke of years. The other man smiled as he recognized them again.

As he recognized them again: his father's hand was encircling the child's fingers, here he comes, the man who gives out the money, the policeman at the corner salutes, and the landlord swears and threatens him with his fist; in the evening, the garden, the table lanterns are lit and from the meadows there arises . . .

The other man's mouth moved and he tried repeating it but without producing a sound. He felt the taste of the words and the silence was unapproachable.

Quick and distant, was what the teacher wrote under his essay. Why does the student not sum up the story?

The other man smiled more broadly, looked at what was coming, and said nothing. He was reading his earliest books, fairy tales and adventures, his mother's face, distant and beautiful and yet severe in his memory. A fat man presents him with his diploma and many nocturnal conversations take place in the twenty-year-old's heart. Twilight, and the lamp is alight, his pen glides across the paper, he was writing and writing, until suddenly everything was cut off and the sirens wailed, the churches were overflowing with prayers for victory, Lord, bless our weapons. The faces of the dying. "Mother," they said. Shot in the abdomen and splinters in the brain, the last obscene word in death, three salvos, people built monuments and the sky had grown completely white. The men were spitting and the women were frightened like everybody else, and it was terrible. The U-boat dived, was blind, and was only listening like an animal in the night; who's coming? And they sat in the cellars, and were blind and listening; what's going to happen now? And then the bombing raid, everything covered in a white haze, a dense white fog, wonderful, and . . .

And Maria was there again, and they were eating breakfast in the garden, the birds were singing, my God, they were singing in the trees, as if paradise had begun, and a year later Maria was dead. He couldn't believe it, how can it suddenly be all over, it's just not possible, but of course it was possible. He had stood at the graveside, three handfuls of earth and the pastor said something and no one heard it. And now Maria is back again?

"Maria is back again," said the other man and saw the white light close in front of him.

"Back again," he said. "And what about me?"

Was he already there, there at last? Where was this "there," actually? It was not important. He just looked at the light as it plunged down. Nothing more. There was nothing more to do.

For the first time in his life there was nothing more to do. Not even the Great I Am wanted anything. He just let it be known that he could be seen.

The other man lay in the corner of the dinghy and looked and waited. Am I really still waiting? He thought about it for a long time.

When he knew it and had seen it, he said, "Yes."

"I am very tired," he said, no longer into the light.

"Then have a nice sleep," said Maria, "you can sleep in tomorrow, as long as you like."

"Yes," said the other man.

He fell asleep at once. The last thing he felt was how tired he was.

The sun was low on the horizon. The underside of its orb would probably soon touch the water. The dinghy was following unerringly the fiery track that the sun was casting on the water.

The evening cumuli were already appearing in the east. But the stars had not yet come out.

The other man lay in the corner of the dinghy. His right hand was hanging overboard in the water, as though he wanted to put it into the tepid water so that it would not be cold any more. The half-smoked cigarette still stuck fast to the corner of his mouth, charred and burned out.

The dinghy was floating imperceptibly towards the night and went further and further away. The surface fishes were jumping in the late light and the sky was plunging into the colors of sunset. Three dolphins were headed directly for the dinghy. Their wake glowed phosphorescently. Just before they reached the floating object, they veered off and looked with astonishment at the dark thing that was in their way, floating on the surface.

Then it was dead calm once more.

The stars came out with an abrupt suddenness, as though

they had been conjured up by magic. Little shooting stars flared up and went out again, as fast as ever they could.

At 2010:47 local time, a mid-sized comet appeared at latitude 8°36″ north and longitude 27°02″. Astronomers had exactly calculated its appearance beforehand.

However, in view of the circumstances then obtaining and the general war situation, the comet could not be observed from the most favorable observation point in the mid-Atlantic, or measured and investigated, although it had remained visible for a long time. In this way, science was deprived of some possibly valuable results affecting some special questions about comets.

Thus the comet was extinguished again without anyone's (presumably also people outside the specialist world of astronomy) having seen it in all its beauty.

In the meantime, the night had grown deep blue. The moon was also rising, its crescent had widened a little. The sea lay unchanged and motionless. The horizon had grown strangely light in the east as well and could be clearly distinguished. The horizon was clear and unobscured. The sun rose next morning, as it had been accustomed to do from time immemorial, and burned down on the motionless sea with all the strength at its disposal. During the day there was a light haze on the horizon.

When the sun sank back into the sea in the evening, as it had been accustomed to do from time immemorial, the dinghy also disappeared over the horizon, as though there had never been anything there. Then the stars came out again, suddenly and magically.